"What are you trying to hide?"

"Hide?" Leida looked at him sharply. "What makes you think I have anything to hide?"

"Do you?" He'd called her bluff.

"Everybody has something to hide," she tossed back lightly. "There's a skeleton in every family closet."

Grant's searching stare wouldn't relent. "What skeleton is hiding in *your* closet, Leida Adams?"

"That's none of *your* business, Senator Hunter."

"Your skeleton wouldn't by any chance be a husband you haven't told me about?"

"Certainly not!"

An unreasonable anger swelled up in Leida like the surging of an evening tide. What right did he have to pry in her private affairs, anyway? He'd saved her from drowning, and for that she was grateful. But she wasn't obligated to spill out to him the story of her life!

Dear Reader:

Romance offers us all so much. It makes us "walk on sunshine." It gives us hope. It takes us out of our own lives, encouraging us to reach out to others. Janet Dailey is fond of saying that romance is a state of mind, that it could happen anywhere. Yet nowhere does romance seem to be as good as when it happens *here*.

Starting in February 1986, Silhouette Special Edition is featuring the AMERICAN TRIBUTE—a tribute to America, where romance has never been so wonderful. For six consecutive months, one out of every six Special Editions will be an episode in the AMERICAN TRIBUTE, a portrait of the lives of six women, all from Oklahoma. Look for the first book, *Love's Haunting Refrain* by Ada Steward, as well as stories by other favorites—Jeanne Stephens, Gena Dalton, Elaine Camp and Renee Roszel. You'll know the AMERICAN TRIBUTE by its patriotic stripe under the Silhouette Special Edition border.

AMERICAN TRIBUTE—six women, six stories, starting in February.

AMERICAN TRIBUTE—one of the reasons Silhouette Special Edition is just that—Special.

The Editors at Silhouette Books

PATTI BECKMAN
Summer's Storm

Silhouette Special Edition

Published by Silhouette Books New York

America's Publisher of Contemporary Romance

SILHOUETTE BOOKS
300 East 42nd St., New York, N.Y. 10017

ISBN: 0-373-09321-7

First Silhouette Books printing July 1986

America's Publisher of Contemporary Romance

Printed in the U.S.A.

Books by Patti Beckman

Silhouette Romance

Captive Heart #8
The Beachcomber #37
Louisiana Lady #54
Angry Lover #72
Love's Treacherous Journey #96
Spotlight to Fame #124
Daring Encounter #154
Mermaid's Touch #179
Forbidden Affair #227
Time For Us #273
On Stage #348

Silhouette Special Edition

Bitter Victory #13
Tender Deception #61
Enchanted Surrender #85
Thunder at Dawn #109
Storm Over the Everglades #169
Nashville Blues #212
The Movie #226
Odds Against Tomorrow #270
Dateline: Washington #278
Summer's Storm #321

PATTI BECKMAN'S

interesting locales and spirited characters will thoroughly delight her reading audience. She lives along the coast of Texas with her husband Charles and their young daughter.

TEXAS

MEXICO

Chapter One

Leida Adams was drowning. She experienced a terrible sense of suffocation, and desperation drove her to struggle. But which way was up? She could see nothing. The water was dark, oppressive—and terrifying.

Blackness began to close in. Panic started to overwhelm her. Then suddenly, when she could stand the constricting agony no longer, she sucked in her breath—and breathed air!

She'd made it to the surface just in time. She coughed violently, choking on salty seawater.

The raging storm blinded her while the furious wind howled like a giant, tortured beast. Around her, the water of the Gulf of Mexico churned wildly as if being plundered by a mad enemy.

Leida tried to swim, fighting against the hopeless odds of giant waves and the beating rain. Her hand struck something hard. It was her sailboat, turned upside down! She clutched frantically at the slippery surface, clinging to it. She was exhausted. Was she to die here, today, this minute?

She wondered vaguely if she had the strength left to survive. Fatigue made her arms unbearably heavy.

She tried to feel along the edge of the Sea Snark for a rope to hold on to. With a sudden, violent jerk the prow of the craft lurched up and struck her under the chin. Her teeth bit into her tongue and she felt a stinging pain. Then the vessel swung around and struck her right shin, sending shock waves up her leg. She cried out, but knew that her voice couldn't be heard above the noise of the storm.

She gasped between the slaps of each deadly wave as she clung tenuously to her tiny craft. She was growing weaker; her muscles ached and her right leg throbbed. The wild expression in her desperate blue eyes only hinted of the terror she felt churning inside her. Which way was land? How far was it?

For an instant she felt a crazy impulse to let go of the craft and swim her way to safety. She'd always been fast and skillful in the water. But sanity overcame the blind panic. As dreadful as the prospect seemed, her best bet was to cling to her boat, praying that by some miracle it would wash ashore, taking her with it.

Another monstrous wave rolled over her, flinging her dark hair into her face, blinding her. She tossed her head back, gasping for air, fighting the raging water with all her might.

Leida couldn't tell how long she battled the rampaging storm. Any sense of time had been swept away with the whitecapped waves that churned about her, tossing her slender body savagely in the waters.

It was growing dark. Leida wondered deliriously how much longer she could hold on. Then gradually the rain subsided and hope stirred in her heart for an instant. With a renewed sense of purpose, she tightened her grip on the boat, determined not to allow fatigue to finish what the storm had been unable to accomplish.

With one hand she struggled to push back the long, tangled tendrils of hair that half blinded her and attempted to peer through the dwindling rain. She could see nothing. Her hope flickered out. Maybe it didn't matter, she thought feebly. She was too exhausted to care much anymore.

Feeling more dead than alive, and not really caring which she was, Leida held on to her boat more through instinct than from any conscious effort to survive.

Finally, the rain stopped altogether. Leida floated with her tiny craft over the waves, which were returning to a calmer state. She drifted in and out of a semiconsciousness that protected her from the stark reality of her plight. At one point, she glanced heavenward with dazed eyes and saw a full moon flashing its pale light between fragmented clouds.

The sea rocked gently, lulling Leida into a sense of well-being. She could almost recall being rocked in her mother's loving arms, hearing the distant sound of a voice piercing the calm. She didn't realize sea gulls were swarming over an offshore oil rig, squalling their forlorn cry of hunger.

She no longer floated, but it didn't matter. She was too weary to open her eyes.

Only a short while ago, the weekend had begun in routine fashion. After work each Friday, Leida would hurry away from the city and head for the Texas Gulf Coast. Her job at a newspaper in Austin provided the income she needed for her real love, painting.

And on the Texas Gulf Coast there was no lack of subjects for her to splash in vivid colors on her canvases. She loved the colorful ambience of the waterfront with its string of shrimp and pleasure boats. Shrimpers with their weathered, lined faces fascinated her. There were stories of hard work and continuing challenges against the elements etched on those faces.

Leida had painted the fishermen and she painted primitive, weather-beaten beach houses, sand dunes turned golden in the hot sunlight, as well. Driftwood, twisted into surrealistic shapes and coated with a silvery patina, the hulk of a wrecked ship, a lonely seabird perched on a barnacle-encrusted piling, a fragile seashell—all were subjects for her brush.

Next to painting, Leida's second love was sailing. When she was drifting lazily on the gentle crests of the sea, her eyes taking in the panorama around her, she could relax; she was away from the work-harried world.

So, each weekend, Leida would escape the city to go to the coast. This weekend, she'd left Austin around the usual time on Friday and driven to the quaint old houseboat she rented for her weekend jaunts.

After spending Saturday and most of Sunday morning painting, she'd decided to treat herself and go sailing. When she'd set out Sunday afternoon in her small ten-foot sailboat, the South Texas sky had been a clear azure. There had been a cluster of dark clouds on the distant horizon, but she'd foolishly chosen to ignore them. In a dreamy, half-dozing state, she'd drifted into the gulf, not aware that the misty coastline had vanished completely and that the threatening storm clouds had mushroomed.

It had been a careless thing to do, she thought darkly. She'd lain back for a while, resting comfortably on the soft cushions she carried with her, and she'd fallen asleep. The sunscreen she wore kept her from burning to a crisp in the blistering South Texas sun, but due to her dozing, she'd missed the sudden change in the temperament of the sky.

Then a raindrop hitting her forehead brought her into full consciousness. She sat erect, looked around and for a moment was totally disoriented. She could see no land. The horizon for 360 degrees was the sea.

At first she felt no panic, only a slight irritation at herself for being so careless. The direction of the wind told her how she must adjust her sail and rudder to head back to land. The first rumble of thunder added a touch of urgency.

Yes, there was a squall brewing. But she felt in no danger. She assured herself that she would be safely back in her cove before she was in any danger.

The boiling clouds picked up speed and the wind started to rise. The swells grew higher, becoming foam-flecked. The scattered raindrops turned into a downpour. And then, before she had sighted land, the storm struck with all its pent-up fury, trapping her in its clutches.

She pulled at the line on her Sea Snark and sent the sail on the craft flipping in the opposite direction. This was no time to panic, she thought. With luck she'd make shore before the lightning began flashing. She tacked into the wind, groaning at the snaillike progress she made.

The waves grew angrier, their whitecaps lashing at the sides of her small boat. The wind gusted, tearing at her hair as if it had a personal vendetta against her. The wind ripped at the sail as the canvas strained to hold the furious bursts of air.

Leida rubbed the back of one arm across her forehead to brush aside the strands of dark brown hair whipped into her face by the gale. Her fingers ached trying to hold the boat's tiller steady. She felt frantic, busily guiding the craft, turning the sail back and forth while trying to keep the salty sea spray out of her eyes.

Anxiously, she glanced past the prow of the boat, scanning the horizon for sight of land. But she'd been tossed out to sea, cut off from the shore by the menacing storm that marched relentlessly toward her.

Her life jacket! What had she done with her life jacket? She cast troubled eyes behind her, but her tiny vessel was devoid of everything except the churning lurch of seawater as it filled up around her. Her heart sank miserably. Then, she saw the bright orange life jacket floating just beyond her reach. She lunged for it, but slipped as her fingers almost curled around the woven belt, and fell headlong into the boat, striking the bottom with her knees. She cried out as a treacherous wave pulled the jacket from her and sent it swirling away on the top of a giant swell. Tears came to her eyes. Should she try to swim after it? Another crash against her back convinced her not to try—she'd never make it.

Just then a thunderous clap shattered the heavens and a pelting rain began to beat down on her. It increased steadily, the wind driving it like needles into her skin. She fought to keep her vision clear, but the rain poured, pounding into her face, filling her boat.

Near-panic gripped her. She had to do something. Immediately. Without thinking, she stood up. A wall of water crashed into her, and she fell out of the boat, sinking beneath the water.

Grant Hunter stood at the bay window in the living room of his seacoast cottage. The casual observer would hardly have called Grant's waterfront house a cottage. The deeply sloping roof capped walls of redwood and imported stone. There was a large deck all around, and the entire house stood on huge pillars, as did all the structures in this subdivision. Summer hurricanes and storms often drove the destructive waves several feet above their normal level, and the pilings kept the buildings safe from the ravages of the boiling water.

Grant paced impatiently. He needed to helicopter out to an oil rig he owned not far offshore to check on problems they were having. But a powerful summer squall had blown in unexpectedly and Grant had been forced to wait it out.

Slender fingers slipped around Grant's arm, giving him a reassuring squeeze. He turned to look into clear, luminous eyes, so transparent their green color almost faded into yellow. The lovely, stylish young woman beside him was Alice Townsend, his fiancée. "Relax, Grant," she said, "the storm will pass."

Grant smiled. Yes, the storm would pass. But when would his own private storm pass? It wasn't just impatience with the weather that made him so restless. The nagging feeling that something was slightly out of kilter had been bothering him for some time now. It was like an invisible bloodhound sniffing at his heels.

His discomfort could be due to the pressures of the upcoming election, he knew. He'd beaten his opponent for the Texas state senate by a narrow margin at the last election. Now, after four years in the senate, he'd grudgingly admitted his father was right. He *was* cut out for a political career. He didn't want it to end. There was still too much he wanted to accomplish.

There had been a time, in his early twenties, when he and his father, Carl Hunter, had become estranged. The Hunters, rich and powerful, were the Kennedys of Texas, and Carl had great political ambitions for his son. Carl Hunter reigned over a vast empire of cattle, oil and shipping wealth. He was accustomed to giving orders and having them obeyed without question. But in Grant, he had sired a young maverick who took orders from no one.

Their relationship had become a battle of wills, a clash of two strong personalities. One day, in his twenty-first year, Grant had walked out on all of it—the vast ranches to which he was heir, the unlimited charge accounts, the Ivy League colleges. With just his clothes on his back and twenty dollars in his pocket, he had hitchhiked to Galveston, gotten a job on a boat going to South America, and from there had worked his way around the world on tramp steamers. He needed time away, time to search for who he really was and what he wanted to make of his life.

A year later, back in the U.S., Grant had roamed the country from the Pacific to the Atlantic. Then, with a newfound maturity, he had returned to college, stubbornly doing it the hard way, working his way through on his own. He received a law degree and became a successful courtroom trial lawyer. Along the way, Grant made smart investments and by now, in his mid-thirties, he had a few oil wells of his own.

Only after he had carved out his own career and proved himself, was he able to go back to Carl Hunter and patch up their family rift. Hunter, glaring at his son while barely able to mask a gleam of pride, had growled, "You're stubborn as an ornery jackass, you know that?"

Grant had glared back. "So are you."

And then Carl could no longer hold back a smile, and they healed the old wounds with the gesture of masculine affection traditional along the Texas-Mexican border—the *embrazo*, patting each other heartily on the back as they embraced.

Carl Hunter could barely disguise his glee when Grant expressed a wish to run for a senate seat in the Texas state legislature, but the older man had learned his lesson. He was not going to be pushy. He knew he must be diplomatic where Grant was concerned. He put his considerable political influence behind Grant, but not in ways that were obvious.

Grant had spent a term in the state senate and now he was having to defend his record, to pit what he'd done against the promises of a challenger. Would the voters recall the bills he'd sponsored as a freshman senator and the committees he'd served on, or would they be swayed by his opponent's promises?

Grant patted the hand on his arm. At least one area of his life was settled. Alice Townsend. His fiancée. He'd known her all his life. Their parents were life-long friends. They'd always known they'd marry someday. And that day would be soon. Officially engaged, they'd started a round of parties and would set the date before long.

The helicopter lifted off the launching pad and rose into the sky. Alice Townsend had flown back to West Texas and Grant was headed for the oil rig out in the gulf. As soon as the storm had died down enough for the chopper to negotiate the gulf safely, Grant had insisted they take off. But only a few hundred yards toward their destination, the craft developed a threatening noise, and the pilot returned to the heli-port.

Grant had to transfer to one of the supply boats that made regular runs between land and the offshore oil rig. Small swells were still churning around them as the boat plowed through the rough waters. Grant stood on the deck, his tall form casting a silhouette over the ropes spread out along behind him.

It was growing dark as the heavily laden boat approached the gigantic oil rig. Grant could hear the familiar, ever-present rumble of the generators and pumps running.

As a youth Grant had worked on his family's cattle ranch, sweating and cursing right along with the hired help, branding cattle and stringing barbed-wire fences. When he was working his way through college, he spent summer vacations toiling on oil rigs as a roughneck, his work clothes covered with grease and grime. The experience had been valuable, and he felt as comfortable drinking a beer and swapping stories with guys down at the local bar as he did while having a martini with a Texas millionaire at an exclusive Dallas country club. He felt his understanding of both life-styles made him a better politician.

When the boat pulled up alongside the rig, the crane operator lowered the birdcage, a small round platform encircled with cables. It was the only way to get from the deck of the boat to the jacked-up oil rig's surface, which was more than seventy-five feet above the water's surface.

Grant stepped onto the edge of the birdcage, grabbing hold of the wire-mesh ring. The collapsible frame lurched up as the crane reeled in the cable, snatching Grant off the boat deck with a sudden snap. His eyes scanned the waves as the birdcage approached the oil rig. The storm clouds had dissipated and an early full moon was bathing the surface of the water with its glistening, silver light.

Suddenly his gaze was riveted to something in the water a few hundred yards from the oil rig. He squinted, his brown eyes intent. Yes, there it was! He could catch glimpses of the object as each swell raised it to the light of the moon. He couldn't be certain at this distance, but it looked like an overturned boat with a human form clinging to it.

"Wait!" he called, motioning to the crane operator to lower the birdcage.

His ascent slowed and then stopped. He signaled again, forcefully, cursing the operator's sluggishness.

Finally, the birdcage reversed direction, and minutes later Grant was once again standing on the deck of the supply boat. He told the captain what he'd seen and the craft sped off.

Grant was positive he'd seen an overturned boat, and he refused to consider turning back until he'd found it. They circled for some time flashing a spotlight into the water before he finally spied the tiny boat riding the lazy crests of the sea.

"There it is!" he shouted above the roar of the engine. He pointed in the right direction. Even as the boat headed toward the craft, Grant pulled off his shoes and slipped out of his jacket. As soon as the boat had pulled alongside the overturned Sea Snark, Grant dived into the water.

Slowly, Leida felt consciousness return. She felt suspended in space, but then memory returned and with it realization. She was still alive. But where was she? She was sure she heard the rumbling sounds of a household coming alive in the morning, but the voices were unfamiliar.

She opened her eyes. This place looked strange. White walls... Where was Kara? A pain shot up toward her knee and she moaned softly. It didn't matter. Closing her eyes, she drifted off to sleep again.

But she slept only moments when she was touched gently on the arm. The rumbling sound returned. She frowned and looked up into a lined, rugged, masculine face.

"Where am I?" she asked. Her voice sounded raspy, faint.

"On the *Hacienda*."

"What's that?"

"An offshore oil rig. This is the infirmary." The man had an unruly mop of rust-red hair. He wore jeans and a T-shirt. "My name's Jess—I'm the medic."

"Oh," she said, smiling. "A doctor."

"Not exactly. More like a paramedic. But a doctor's been called. As soon as you're able, you'll be taken ashore so he can check you over."

As Leida looked around, she realized she was wrapped in warm blankets and a glucose bottle hung on a stand beside her bed. From the bottle a tube ran down to a needle inserted in her left arm. "How did I get here, anyway?" Leida asked. "I remember hanging on to my sailboat on the verge of drowning…then…" Nothing. Or almost nothing. Vaguely, she could recall being swept up in strong, muscular arms, snuggled safely against a man's broad chest, then sinking into unconsciousness.

"I guess you would have drowned if it hadn't been for Senator Hunter." Jess grinned. "He spotted you out there and rescued you."

Leida stared at the young medic. She still felt half-dazed and she wasn't sure she'd heard him correctly. "What—what did you say?"

"I said," the young man repeated patiently, "Senator Hunter rescued you from what story writers call a 'watery grave.' He dived in and hauled you out just before you went under. Guess you could call him a hero."

Leida licked her lips. "Senator Grant Hunter?"

"Yeah. Everybody in Texas knows the senator. He owns this oil rig."

The constant rumble of the generators mingled with a sudden pounding in Leida's brain. *Senator Hunter.* No, it couldn't be!

"You're…sure it was Senator Hunter?" she asked weakly.

The medic gave her a curious look. "Yes. I work for the man."

Leida shook her head slowly. Of all the men in Texas, she had to be rescued by Senator Grant Hunter. This had all the makings of a grade-B movie.

If Senator Grant Hunter had known whom he was rescuing, he would have tossed her back in the gulf to drown!

Leida worked as a political cartoonist for a newspaper in Austin. She had started doing the illustrations for the newspaper's editorial page several months ago when their regular cartoonist resigned. It began as a temporary assignment, but her drawings had a unique style that immediately attracted statewide attention. Her editor was delighted.

Sometimes editorial writers on the paper suggested ideas for the biting, satirical cartoons, and sometimes the cartoons were vehicles for her own social and political views. At first she had been uncertain about this more commercial turn in her career, but then she began to enjoy it. And there had been a substantial increase in her paycheck that was going to help her eventually realize her dream of working full-time on more serious painting.

Her editor thought the cartoons should have a masculine byline and came up with the pseudonym, Alex Carter. Leida welcomed the anonymity. In fact, she stipulated that she would draw for the editorial page only if the newspaper guaranteed to keep her identity a secret. The cartoons reflected the often controversial editorial views of the paper and were a hot political item, drawing a lot of mail. Once Leida's work was published, letters poured in—some of them applauded her views while others expressed a view that Alex Carter ought to be tarred and feathered and run out of the state.

Leida was well aware of the steamy nature of Texas politics. Feelings often ran high during a political race; mudslinging and personal insults were not uncommon. Her newspaper was known all over the state for its outspoken political stand. Editorial writers didn't mince words and, as a consequence, the cartoons used had a blistering, biased nature. Any political figure the newspaper didn't like appeared in the cartoons as a simpleminded buffoon or a blackhearted villain, his features distorted into a grotesque caricature.

And the newspaper did not like Grant Hunter.

Early in the senatorial race, the newspaper had endorsed his opponent, then it had gone after Grant Hunter with an editorial vengeance. Leida could imagine that it was a real thorn in the senator's political side.

Leida's cartoons poked fun at many social and political idiocies, both on a state and a national level. But, in agreement with the newspaper's editorial policy, one of her cartoon's chief targets had been Senator Grant Hunter of the Texas state legislative body in Austin. The "Alex Carter" drawings had become a symbol for the opposition to the senator. Her caricatures had made a mockery out of his rugged, handsome features, turning them into gargoylelike distortions.

And now she had been rescued from drowning by the very man she'd been lambasting in her cartoons! She felt her cheeks growing red with embarrassment.

The door to the offshore drilling rig's medical facility opened. A broad-shouldered man filled the doorway. "Well, how's our patient?" he asked in a rich baritone voice.

Leida stared wide-eyed at Grant Hunter. She pulled the cover closer around her chin, wishing she could sink into the pillows.

Chapter Two

Grant Hunter crossed the room, swung a chair around and sat astride it, resting his broad hands on the back as he gazed thoughtfully at her.

Leida had the sensation that all of the Texas outdoors had come in with him. The strong, suntanned hands resting on the chair back looked as if they were used to gripping a horse's reins. She had seen him before—several times, in fact—but always from the distance of her seat in the visitors' gallery in the state legislature. A powerfully built man in his mid-thirties, he had a resonant voice that easily filled the senate chambers.

She was not quite prepared for the sensation of his presence up close. She felt an almost physical impact from his intense brown-eyed gaze. The man radiated a charge of energy that seemed to make the air crackle. It was not difficult to see how he could mesmerize a group of constituents at a voters' rally. Whatever her newspaper thought of him politically, there was certainly no discounting the man's towering personality.

"Well, I'd say you had a close call."

"Yes," she murmured. "I nearly drowned. I guess I would have if it hadn't been for you. Jess told me what happened—that you dived in and rescued me. I don't know what to say except thank you."

He waved her gratitude aside with a smile. "There's no need for thanks," he murmured. "I'm grateful that I was able to get to you in time." Then, looking somewhat stern, he asked, "What were you doing way out here in the gulf anyway? You had no business being this far from shore in that eggshell of a sailboat."

"I know," she admitted, feeling foolish. "It started out as such a nice day, but it got hot and I must have dozed off. I hadn't realized how far I'd gone."

"Well," he said smiling, "we've done all we can for you here. As soon as we got you on the rig, we radioed our company doctor. He advised Jess to move you as little as possible in case something was broken and to wrap you in warm blankets and start a glucose IV to prevent you from going into shock. But we need to get you ashore for a more complete examination."

"Please don't go to any more trouble over me. I'm all right—"

"We'll let the doctor be the judge of that. My helicopter was tied up for a couple of hours for some repairs, but it's okay now and just landed on the deck.

We're going to fly you ashore." Then he asked, "Do you have a family you want us to notify?"

Leida shook her head.

He continued looking at her with an intense, searching gaze that somehow unnerved her. Had he made the connection between her and the political cartoonist, Alex Carter? But that was impossible!

"What's your name?" he asked.

"Leida Adams."

"Miss...? Mrs....?"

"Miss."

Again he smiled and the warmth in his brown eyes sent tingles down her spine. "Leida. A very pretty name. I'm Grant Hunter, Miss Adams."

"Yes, I know," she said, wishing she could somehow dissolve out of sight into the pillow.

"Well, Leida Adams," he said, arising briskly. "Get ready for a helicopter ride."

The next thing she knew, two husky oil-rig workers were transferring her to a stretcher with unexpected gentleness.

The flight in the noisy aircraft took only minutes. She expected an ambulance to be waiting to take her to a hospital. Instead, the chopper landed in a fenced area beside a luxurious beach home.

They were met by some men who worked for Grant. Her stretcher was carried upstairs to a bedroom where a doctor and registered nurse were waiting.

Grant had accompanied her on the flight back to his summer resort home. He followed her stretcher into the room. "Miss Adams, this is our company physician, Dr. Sanders. I'll leave you in his capable hands."

With that he withdrew from the room, gently closing the door after him.

The physician was a man in his late thirties with thinning, sandy hair. His piercing blue eyes gazed at her through silver-framed glasses.

"Well, Miss Adams," he said, "I understand you have been through quite an ordeal. Let's have a look at you."

He unwrapped the blankets in which Leida had been swaddled and, after careful probing, he said cheerfully, "Nothing appears to be broken. I told Jess not to move you any more than absolutely necessary in case of a fracture somewhere. So they left you in your clothes and wrapped you in blankets. But I'm sure you must be uncomfortable in those damp things. Nurse Evans here will help you change into something more suitable."

The doctor left the room briefly while Leida slipped out of the garments she had worn on her boating trip and into a nightgown. When the doctor returned, he did some more checking, using a light to look into her eyes, listening to her chest with his stethoscope.

"I'm all right, really," Leida protested. "I told Senator Hunter there wasn't any need to make a big deal out of this. I just want to go home."

"Where's home."

"I live in Austin—"

"You drove down for the weekend?"

She nodded.

The doctor removed his stethoscope, folded it into his bag. "Don't think you're up to a drive like that quite yet. Let me get Grant back in here."

He went out in the hallway and spoke to someone. In a few minutes he returned with Grant Hunter. The two men stood near the foot of the bed. "Just looking her over, Grant, I don't think there's any serious damage," the doctor explained. "Nasty bruise on the chin and leg. Mostly, she's suffering from exhaustion and exposure."

Leida struggled to a sitting position. For a moment, the room swam, but she grimly forced herself to remain sitting. "Look, I really appreciate all the trouble you've gone to for me, Senator Hunter, but I'm quite all right. I'm able to get up and go home."

The doctor frowned. "I wouldn't want her out of bed just yet. She needs a day or two of rest, then a gradual resumption of activities."

"Then that's what she'll have!" Grant Hunter said. "We'll keep her right here with a nurse."

"No!" Leida exclaimed, horrified at the prospect of spending a night as the houseguest of the senator. "I'm not going to impose on you any longer—"

"Nonsense," Hunter said in a tone that closed the matter.

Leida wanted to argue the point, but she knew the doctor's recommendation was probably right. She was exhausted. She slid back down underneath the blankets. Faintly, as the two men left the room, she heard the doctor saying, "She's young, strong and healthy. If she rests for a day or two, she'll be good as new...."

The voice faded like a radio station going off the air. Leida gave a relaxed sigh and fell into a deep sleep filled with dreams of seafaring Vikings, all of whom resembled Grant Hunter.

"Good morning."

The cheerful voice probed sleepy depths from which Leida reluctantly emerged. She stretched, lingering for a moment in a drowsy state between waking and sleeping. The fragrance of coffee and bacon brought her fully awake.

For a moment she was confused by her surroundings. Then she recognized Dr. Sanders's nurse standing beside her bed. She glanced around the room and remembered with a feeling of dismay that she was a houseguest of Senator Grant Hunter.

"How's our sleepyhead today?" asked the nurse.

Leida's gaze fell on the bedside tray from which emanated the delicious aromas of steaming coffee and crisp bacon. "Hungry," she murmured, pulling herself to a sitting position.

"That's a good sign." The nurse smiled. "Breakfast in a minute. First a check of vital signs."

Before Leida could say anything, a thermometer was thrust in her mouth. Then the nurse bustled around, taking her blood pressure and counting her pulse. "You slept the clock around," she said cheerfully.

"Mmm?" Leida mumbled around the thermometer with sudden panic.

The nurse removed the thermometer, frowned at it. "Umm. Normal. Blood pressure, pulse rate all normal. Very good."

"You said I slept the clock around. What day is this?" Leida demanded.

"Tuesday."

"Good Lord!" Leida exclaimed. She had gone boating on Sunday, planning to return to Austin Sunday night so she could be at work Monday morning. Here it was Tuesday. Her editor would be furious.

"I've got to go!" she gasped, throwing back the covers. She swung her feet to the floor.

"Hey, not so fast," the nurse warned.

Sitting on the edge of the bed, Leida felt her head balloon. The room tilted.

"You're not going anywhere until you've had some breakfast," the nurse said severely.

Leida couldn't seem to manage an argument. There was a big, empty hole where her stomach should have been.

When the nurse, whose name was Margaret Baker, placed breakfast in front of Leida, she wolfed down bacon, eggs and fruit, plus several cups of strong coffee. After that, she felt strength returning to her legs.

"Now we'll see about taking those first steps," Margaret said, as she helped Leida to a nearby chair.

Leida was then able to take some more steps to the bathroom under her own power. She took a shower, scrubbed her face and applied makeup. She found her clothes, the shorts and halter top that she'd worn on her ill-fated sailing trip, laundered and neatly folded on the lavatory counter top. She dressed, feeling more like her normal self by the minute, although still somewhat shaky.

When she returned to the bedroom, Margaret nodded her approval. "You're looking so much better,

Leida. Dr. Sanders will be pleased. He's coming by in a little bit to check on you.''

"A doctor who makes house calls?"

A smile of amusement tugged at the nurse's lips. "He's employed by Hunter Industries, their company doctor. He goes wherever Senator Hunter needs him.''

"Well, I have to get to a telephone. I have to call my boss to see if I have a job left.''

"You stay right there. I'll bring the telephone to you.''

Margaret left the room, returning minutes later with a telephone that she plugged into a wall terminal, then handed the instrument to Leida.

Using her credit card number, Leida charged the long distance call to her home phone in Austin. In no time, she was connected with her editor, Sam Daniels.

"Where in blazes are you, Leida?" Daniels fumed. "Why weren't you in the office yesterday?"

"I was almost at the bottom of the gulf," Leida explained. Briefly, she described her boating accident, leaving out the name of her rescuer.

"Damn!" The editor gasped. "That's terrible, Leida. I'm sorry. Are you all right now?"

"Yes, just a little shaky.''

"Where are you?"

Leida suppressed a smile. "You wouldn't believe me if I told you. Look, Sam, I'll be back late today or tomorrow, okay?"

"You take all the time you need, Leida. Take the rest of the week if necessary!"

Shortly after that, Dr. Sanders arrived. After another thorough examination, he looked satisfied. "Just as I thought; nothing wrong that a good rest couldn't repair. Now you can start resuming your normal activities, Miss Adams, but do it slowly or you'll find yourself back in bed. Walk around the room a bit this morning. After lunch you may go downstairs. If you feel tired or get a little shaky, sit down. By tomorrow, you should be pretty much back to normal."

Nurse Margaret Baker stayed until noon. By then, Leida had met the other member of the household, Mrs. Garcia, the housekeeper, who bustled upstairs with a lunch tray laden with an authentic Mexican meal—enchiladas, refried beans, guacamole salad.

"You like Mexican food, miss?" Mrs. Garcia asked, arranging the meal on a table beside the window.

"Love it," Leida exclaimed.

"Good," the housekeeper said, beaming. "It will make you strong again. My husband, Joe, he works for Mr. Hunter on the oil rigs. He says it's the frijole beans and jalapeno peppers that make him strong."

On the way out of the room, she paused in the doorway, fanning herself with her apron. "Mr. Hunter, he's been out at the oil rig all morning, but he called to see how you are. He'll be home in a little while."

Leida felt her stomach sink. She didn't relish the prospect of another awkward meeting with Senator Grant Hunter. The doctor said she could go downstairs after lunch. Perhaps she could quietly sneak away, though how she could get back to her houseboat and her car, several miles up the coast, she didn't know. Her sailboat had been wrecked and she had no money.

She put aside her problems for the moment and enjoyed the tangy Mexican dishes. The size of her appetite surprised her. She thought it was probably nature's way of restoring her strength.

Mrs. Garcia had brought her a San Antonio morning newspaper with the meal. After finishing lunch, Leida glanced through the paper. When she reached the editorial page, she was dismayed to see her latest cartoon. The Alex Carter political cartoons had become so popular that they were being syndicated to other newspapers in the state. This one was an especially ludicrous caricature of Senator Grant Hunter, depicting him in a big Cadillac with steer horns on the hood, enormous diamonds on his fingers, smoking a huge cigar, driving through a ghetto neighborhood on his way to the country club, completely oblivious to the poor people scrambling out of the way of his car, which was labeled "The Hunter Political Machine."

"Not very flattering, is it?" a baritone voice murmured behind her.

She swung around with a gasp.

"Sorry, Miss Adams," Grant apologized. "I didn't mean to startle you."

The newspaper was suddenly scorching her fingers. She tried to stuff it beside her, out of sight. "G-good morning," she stammered.

He took a seat in a chair facing her. His brown-eyed gaze engulfed her. She had a momentary feeling that she was drowning again. He smiled warmly. "You look terrific!"

Her hand moved to the hair brushing her shoulder in an instinctive, self-conscious gesture. Her cheeks felt warm. "Thank you."

His gaze continued to sweep over her features. "Last time I saw you, you resembled a nearly drowned kitten." He chuckled. "You've made quite a transformation."

"I—I must have looked a mess," she admitted.

"Yes, but you're so much better. The color is back in your cheeks, your eyes are bright. I thought you were pretty when we rescued you. I believe I'll have to revise that to beautiful."

Leida swallowed with some difficulty. His words seemed to be sincere. It was disconcerting how this man always seemed to scatter her emotions in all directions.

"I spoke with Dr. Sanders," Grant went on. "He's very pleased with your condition."

"Yes, he says I can resume normal activities. So I'll be on my way. I don't know how to express my gratitude, Senator Hunter, for all you've done...not only saving my life, but providing me with medical care, the hospitality of your home. If there's any way I can repay you—"

"You've already thanked me," Grant interrupted her. "As for repayment, seeing you recovered is all the repayment I want. And about what you said, being on your way. I wouldn't be in too big a hurry about that. Dr. Sanders told me you're going to be pretty shaky on your feet for another day or two. I think you should stay until tomorrow. Mrs. Garcia will be here to look after you. I'll be spending the night out at the oil rig.''

Then he leaned forward and retrieved the newspaper from beside her. ''Mind if I have another look at that?''

Leida felt a heat wave spreading up her face to her hairline as Grant studied her cartoon. ''That Alex Carter really has it in for me,'' he muttered, shaking his head. ''He's launched a regular vendetta against me. Look at that!''

Leida nodded numbly, wishing she could somehow turn invisible.

''On top of it, he's a lousy cartoonist, don't you think?''

She felt a sudden reversal of her emotions. ''What do you mean by that?'' she asked testily.

''He can't draw.''

Now her embarrassment was replaced by rising irritation. He'd just pricked her professional pride.

''Well, I wouldn't say that,'' she exclaimed. ''I can see where it would make you angry, but the artwork is good.''

Grant scowled at the drawing again. ''You honestly think so?''

Suddenly, Leida's momentary flash of anger dissolved as she saw the humor in the situation. She pictured the expression that would cross Grant's face if she told him he was sitting not two feet away from the cartoonist who drew the picture!

''Let me have another look at that,'' she said, taking the paper from him. She held it up, her gaze moving from the caricature to Grant's face. She could no longer keep from giggling. "Looks just like you!" she exclaimed.

He gave her a peculiar look, then his face broke into a broad grin. "I guess I should try to keep a sense of humor about these things," Hunter said ruefully. "It's just that Alex Carter and that editorial bunch on the Austin paper he works for are unfair. I'm not the person in those cartoons at all. And, frankly, they're not helping me one bit in the coming election. People tend to be influenced by stuff like this."

Then he tossed the newspaper aside. "To heck with politics. I'm not going to bore you with that. What say we take a stroll downstairs to the beach? Doc Sanders said it would be okay if you get out a bit. And I thought you'd like to have a look at your sailboat."

"My sailboat?" she gasped. "You mean you rescued that, too?"

He nodded. "We tied it to the boat and brought it back with us. The hull looks okay, but I'm afraid the sail looks like a lace curtain."

"Oh, I'm so happy!" she cried, clapping her hands. "I love that little boat."

"Even if it nearly drowned you?"

"That wasn't the boat's fault. It was my own foolishness!"

Chapter Three

The sun glinted off Leida's curly, dark brown hair. She stood beside Grant at the water's edge, her emotions disturbed by his presence.

Leida had insisted on inspecting her boat. Grant had taken her arm and had helped her down the stairs of his house and toward the emerald gulf. She'd been aware of his piney after-shave lotion, his thick brown hair, the way the muscles in his arms knotted as he kept a firm hold on her in case she stumbled.

What's going on here? she'd asked herself. What was causing her senses to sharpen so acutely? What made her flesh tingle, her heart beat faster?

Politics aside, Senator Grant Hunter was a most attractive man. She attributed her unsettling emotional state to that—a normal response to a strong male's presence.

She looked away so he couldn't see her eyes. The sky was a clear azure today. There was no hint of the recent furious storm. Sailboats dotted the horizon, their white sails glistening in the pristine air. She sucked in her breath, the fragrant salt air filling her lungs.

For a few minutes, the memory of her recent escape from drowning came to mind and she felt a little sick. Her knees almost buckled. But she had always been a survivor; a dark memory of another chapter in her life, better forgotten, reminded her of that. The ghosts of old memories brought a sudden clammy chill. Resolutely, she pushed them aside. She wouldn't have survived back then if she hadn't had an inner core of strength. She could survive this.

That inner strength took over now. She swallowed hard, dismissed the quaking feeling that threatened to overwhelm her, and chatted gaily to mask the lingering uneasiness she refused to acknowledge.

Her small boat was docked at a pier behind Grant's house. They walked to it.

"What's left of my sail wouldn't make a good dust rag," she said ruefully.

"It took a real beating," Grant agreed. He bent down and lifted one ragged edge of the small piece of cloth that remained. He looked at her. "I'm surprised you were able to hang on as long as you did."

Leida smiled weakly. It was frightening to realize how close she'd come to dying out there in the watery depths of the Gulf of Mexico. A shudder ran through her.

"I—I'd rather put those thoughts out of my mind. I don't want to think about it."

"There's no need to dwell on it," Grant said, standing. "The main thing is to get your boat back in operation. What it needs is a new sail. Everything else seems to be intact. If you feel like it, I'll drive you into town and we can pick out a replacement."

"That's very kind of you," she replied. "But I'm sure you have more important things to do."

"What's more important than helping a damsel in distress?" he asked with a touch of old-fashioned Southern gallantry.

"Don't state senators have legislation to draft or bills to work on?" Leida asked lightly.

"Sure, but we take time off, just like real people," Grant teased back.

"I know that. I just mean . . ."

"What?" Grant asked gently.

Leida's expression was disturbed. She bit her lip.

He looked at her steadily, his brown eyes warm and friendly. "Is there a problem?" he asked.

"I don't have any money," she blurted out. "I never take my purse when I go sailing. I wouldn't have any way to pay for it."

He smiled. "If that's all that's bothering you, I can take care of it."

"No, I couldn't allow it!" She was adamant.

Grant studied her face for a minute. As he did, his features softened momentarily. His searching, intent gaze did unsettling things to her. Why was he looking at her that way?

Then he said, "If that bothers you, you can pay me back."

Leida considered for a moment. She was in a quandary. Without her sailboat, she had no way of getting several miles back up the coast to the cove where her houseboat was anchored and her car was parked. Grant would probably drive her back there if she asked him, but that solution made her uneasy. She didn't want him to find out any more information about her—where she lived, her car license—anything that might give him a further clue to her real identity. Politicians as powerful as Grant Hunter had all kinds of sources. It wouldn't take much for him to be able to trace her to her job on the Austin newspaper. For a reason that she wasn't going to analyze at the moment, she didn't want to spoil their growing friendship.

On the other hand, she hated to be indebted to him any further, even temporarily. Again she thought about her scathing political cartoons of him. She cringed inwardly when she remembered her caricatures of him as a lamebrained cowboy on a monstrous horse riding into a Dallas country club, or a bloated oil tycoon, smoking a giant cigar, stomping around a forest of oil derricks. If he knew who she really was, he'd no doubt kick her off his property and let her worry about her own sail. She shouldn't accept his generosity, but after considering her circumstances, she finally concluded that she didn't have much choice.

"All right," she said, then added firmly, "but only on the condition that I pay you back. I'm already in debt to you for saving my life."

"Let's not go into that again," Grant said, dismissing her gratitude. "Do you feel up to a trip into town?"

"Yes," she said, feeling stronger than she had when they'd left his house.

"Are you positive?"

"Yes, I think it would be good for me."

"All right, but if you get tired, just tell me and I'll bring you back. Agreed?"

"Sure," she said.

Grant smiled. She felt herself turn warm all over. She tried to tell herself her reaction was to the heat of the South Texas sun, but had to admit it was more than that. She was beginning to like Grant Hunter. His smile could do very unsettling things to her.

Where was the selfish, political ogre her newspaper had depicted? They'd brainwashed her to the point that she'd expected Grant Hunter to be sporting a set of horns and spiked tail. Instead, she was finding him to be a kind, considerate person, every inch a gentleman. He had plunged into the Gulf to rescue her and had seen that she had the best of care. Was it possible her newspaper was all wrong about him?

Still, her innate sense of caution warned her that some political rascals could be very charming on the surface. She was going to reserve final judgment until she got to know him better. But for now she'd keep an open mind about him.

Grant led Leida off the pier to a carport under the house on its high pilings where he kept a late-model expensive sports car. He helped her in and then left for a moment to tell Mrs. Garcia where he was going. He returned and slid behind the wheel. He started the engine, flipped on the air conditioner and backed out onto a paved road that wound around the plush subdivision.

Grant drove leisurely through the development of elaborate beachfront houses. Palm trees gave the area a tropical atmosphere. As he handled the steering wheel of the powerful sports car, he stole glances at the profile of the lovely young woman seated beside him. She intrigued him. Who was she? Where did she come from?

He guessed her age to be in the mid-twenties, though something about her manner made her seem more mature. He thought there was a depth of character beyond her years that he'd glimpsed in her eyes. And yet when looking at her, he saw the flawless, unblemished complexion of a young woman. And she was lovely—her mouth was full and sensitive, her eyes were fringed with long lashes and she had an abundance of lush, soft brown hair that cascaded around her face and fell to her shoulders.

His gaze, trailing lower, took in the hollow of her throat, lingered a bit on the tantalizing curve of full breasts, then down to a narrow waist and long, beautifully sculptured legs left bare by the shorts she was wearing. Her calves had lovely curves, her ankles were slender.

With an effort, he concentrated on his driving. The delicate, perfumed fragrance of her bath powder and cologne made him intensely aware of her presence in the small car, causing his hands to tremble slightly as he maneuvered the automobile.

She said she wasn't married. Was she telling him the truth? Probably. There was no reason to lie about that. Had she been married? Did she live around here? Dozens of questions about her nagged at him.

She had been silent since they left his house. She appeared to be engrossed in the scenery they were passing.

"Penny for your thoughts," he murmured. "You seem very absorbed in something."

"I was just admiring that tree over there," she said, pointing it out to him. It was a giant old oak tree in a vacant lot near the beach. Its limbs had been twisted into surrealistic shapes by the gulf winds that had buffeted it for decades. "It makes me think of an old man, withered and bent, leaning on a cane, looking heavenward."

Grant chuckled. "Very good metaphor. That old oak is something of a landmark around here. We're involved in a community effort to make that vacant lot into a city park to save the old tree. I've taken a lot of photographs of it. One turned out pretty well. I'm thinking of having it enlarged to hang in my den."

"You're a photographer?"

"Strictly an amateur."

She nodded thoughtfully. "I can see why you'd want to photograph it. I'd like to paint it sometime."

He seized on her words. "Oh, you're an artist?"

She bit her lip, frowning slightly and looking away. She hadn't meant to let that bit of information slip out, he thought. Dammit, why was she being so secretive? What was she hiding?

She shrugged. "Sort of."

"Is that how you make your living?" he pursued. He was determined to find out more about her.

But she was obviously on guard. "Not exactly." She quickly changed the subject. "Oh, there's an interesting scene!" She pointed to a row of trees along the water's edge. They all leaned away from the surf as if throwing hands in front of their faces to protect them from the daily onslaught of the wind against their branches.

Grant was fascinated by the sudden, animated expression on Leida's face. She looked as delighted as a child who had just glimpsed a decorated tree on Christmas morning. Her eyes were bright, her cheeks warm with color. She seemed totally absorbed by what she saw. It made her absolutely adorable.

"Yes, I like that scene, too," he agreed. "But it's not nearly as interesting as the lovely lady sitting here with me. Tell me more about yourself, Leida."

But she was determined to protect her privacy. "There's not much to tell," she said shortly. "You're the one who's had an interesting life, coming from such a prominent family, active in state politics. Is it hard being in the public eye that way?"

"Sometimes. Someone in my position is always under constant scrutiny. No matter how I vote on a bill, the media is apt to jump to the wrong conclusions. I've been painted as a spokesman for the rich, a defender of the privileged class. In fact, what I'm trying to do is help pass legislation that will make it possible for more people to get ahead in this state. Since that can't be done overnight, my opponent is trying to paint me as a blackhearted rascal. Well, you saw that vicious cartoon about me in the morning paper.''

He noticed a strange expression flit across her face, but she immediately covered it up by exclaiming, "Oh, we're coming into town."

Grant stopped at a traffic light. He looked directly at her. "I just got on my soapbox for you. Now I believe it's your turn to tell me something about yourself."

Either she didn't hear or pretended not to. She pointed at a white clapboard building situated at the water's edge next to a long pier. "Is that the boat shop?"

Grant sighed. "Yes," he said, slightly exasperated. Might as well forget about giving her the third degree, he thought. She stonewalled him every time he tried to pry out any information about her personal life.

The tires of his car crunched as they pulled into a shell-covered parking area.

"Let me help you out," he said, switching off the ignition. "Wait till I get around to your side."

"Old-fashioned gallantry?" she teased. "I thought it was out of style."

"You're still recovering, remember?" He moved quickly around the car and opened her door. "I brought you here and I'm responsible for you."

He held her hand to assist her as she stepped out of the car. Her eyes met his for a moment, strangely soft and searching. "You're ... you're a very nice man, Senator Hunter."

He felt the warmth of her fingers in his and he couldn't keep from giving them a squeeze. "You sound surprised," he murmured.

She allowed her fingers to rest in his a moment, then withdrew them with a blush. "It's just that some of the newspaper editorials about you—"

"I know," he said ruefully. "Let me tell you, when a politician gets editorial writers as enemies, they can make him sound like Simon Legree. Do you believe everything you read in the papers?"

She looked flustered. "N-no—of course not."

"Well, anyway," Grant said, smiling, "I think we've become good enough friends by now to dispense with that 'Senator Hunter' stuff, don't you? Let's keep it Leida and Grant, okay?"

She nodded. "Yes. Okay."

They moved from the parking area to the steps going up to the boardwalk around the boat shop. There was the familiar waterfront aroma of saltwater in the humid breeze. Sea gulls circled above them, calling loudly.

In the shop, they asked a clerk for the replacement sail. He went back to a storeroom to locate one. While they waited, Leida and Grant browsed among the fishing poles and tackle, dip nets, waders, surfboards and water skis.

Leida stopped at a counter of Gulf Coast souvenirs. She picked up a doll made from seashells. "This is nice. Looks like a bit of local handcraft."

Grant took the doll from her to examine it more closely. As he did, his hands brushed hers. The touch sent a shock wave of physical awareness through him. He saw a jolt in her suddenly widened eyes and knew she, too, had felt the electric attraction. The chemistry between them could become dangerous, a voice within him warned. For a moment their gaze locked. He saw a play of emotions in the churning brown depths of her eyes—confusion, uncertainty.

His fingers moved over the smooth contours of the doll made from seashells. "You're very sensitive to all kinds of artistic expression, aren't you, Leida?" he said softly.

"Yes. It's important, don't you agree?"

He looked at her again, drawn by her beauty as well as something less tangible. He saw a depth to her that was surprising. What were the secrets locked behind those large eyes?

Grant turned the doll over and saw a stamp on the bottom. He sighed and showed it to her. It read, Made in Taiwan.

She looked sad as she put the doll back on the shelf. "And I'd made up such a wonderful story about a person who spent days searching the beach for just the right shells, fashioning them together with loving care."

"I shouldn't have disillusioned you. I'm sorry."

"Don't be. Life is full of disillusionment. If you can't take it, you flunk."

"You sound like a survivor."

She raised her chin, giving him a defiant look. "You'd better believe it."

"Good for you. It's the survivors who make the grade."

She smiled. The momentary sadness was gone from her eyes. "It's really funny, isn't it? I was getting sentimental over a doll that was probably made on a production line in Taiwan. Just goes to show, Grant—things are not always what they seem."

She had given him a strange look as she had emphasized that last sentence. Was she trying to tell him something about herself? he wondered.

They were interrupted by the clerk who had found the sail they needed. Grant paid for the sail and tucked it under one arm as they headed for the door.

Just as they exited from the front of the shop, some cars and two vans suddenly pulled into the parking lot. Leida saw the emblem of a local television station on the side of the vans. People were piling out of the vehicles and surrounding them. One fellow was loaded down with a TV camera.

"What—what's going on?" Leida gasped.

But before Grant could respond, she found herself engulfed by the onslaught of media people, a camera pointed at her and a microphone stuck in her face.

"Are you the young lady Senator Grant rescued from drowning?" the TV reporter asked her.

Leida was stunned. She stared with disbelief at the reporters, then at Grant.

"How did you people hear about that?" Grant asked. He looked surprised, but his voice was friendly.

A newspaper reporter responded, "Some oil rig operator has been spreading it around the waterfront, Senator. We heard about it just this morning. We called your place, but your housekeeper said you'd come into town. Is the story true, Senator? And if it is, is this the young lady in question?"

Grant looked at Leida. Seeing the stricken expression on her face, he said, "She's not up to interviews yet, fellas. Give her a little time."

"Then it is true?" asked one of the reporters, scribbling quickly.

"What's your name?" one of them asked her.

Leida was horrified. If she wanted to keep her identity a secret, this was not the way to do it!

The reporters were persistent. "How did you feel about being rescued by Senator Hunter?" another person asked. "Had you known him before?"

Leida just looked wide-eyed and shook her head.

"Tell our viewers what it was like to be adrift in the storm. How long had you been clinging to your boat before Senator Hunter arrived on the scene?"

"Senator, we understand you took Miss... Mrs.—"

"Leida," she said, determined to shut them up about who she was. But her first name was all they were going to get from her.

"We understand you took her to your home after the accident. Has she been there ever since?"

"I'm sorry," Grant said firmly. "The lady has been through a lot. I'll issue a statement to the press tomorrow." Grant stepped through the growing crowd and pulled Leida along with him.

The reporters followed. "You're a hero, Senator! This is quite a scoop! At least tell us who she is and where she's from. Her hometown newspaper will want the story."

Leida was growing furious at their persistence. She spun around to face them. "Yes," she said evenly, "the senator saved my life. I'm very grateful. Beyond that I have no comment at this time."

"Please, fellows," Grant responded good-naturedly. "Later. I'll issue a statement later." With that he whisked Leida to his car, stowed the sail in the back seat and quickly helped her in.

No sooner had he closed the door than one of the reporters yelled a question through the window at him. Grant smiled indulgently, waved and nodded, and started the engine. He backed up slowly, avoiding the spectators milling around to see what was exciting enough to call out a bevy of newspeople to the heart of their small town.

On the road back home, Grant seemed to relax. Leida felt a tight knot in her stomach that refused to unwind.

An angry suspicion was growing inside her that the whole thing had been set up by Grant Hunter. SENATOR HUNTER A HERO, RESCUES YOUNG WOMAN. Great headlines for a politician! She remembered how he'd gone in the house to speak to Mrs. Garcia just before they started into town. Had he taken that opportunity to tip off the media? Did he hope to generate some favorable publicity for himself and play up the hero angle? Some politicians would stop at nothing to win votes.

It would play beautifully in the press. Even her editor, Sam Daniels, would have to lay off Grant for a time. Scathing cartoons about a genuine hero would only make the newspaper look bad.

Maybe, she thought angrily, her paper's editorial writers were right. Grant Hunter had fooled her with his kind, courtly manner. Was he, under all that charm, nothing more than a cutthroat politician, after all?

Chapter Four

The sun hung low in the west against the backdrop of a pale pink summer sky. It was almost dark. This time of year darkness descended over the water after eight o'clock.

A tiny Sea Snark with a bright new sail skimmed perkily along the water, as if eager to be safely nestled in its own alcove. The sparkling water of the Gulf of Mexico lay almost sleeping, gently flexing its rippling muscles in tiny waves upon the surface.

Leida was headed home. Grant had insisted she spend the night at his beach house. He'd asked Mrs. Garcia to prepare supper for Leida after he'd installed the new sail. He said he'd see her in the morning, then took the helicopter back to his oil rig.

Once he'd departed, Leida informed Mrs. Garcia of her plans to return home that evening. The housekeeper had shaken her head and clucked her tongue disapprovingly. She predicted Mr. Hunter would be terribly upset, but Leida was adamant.

She'd boarded her tiny craft nervously, feeling a bit skittish after her boating mishap. But she was determined not to let such an accident deter her from sailing. She'd forget the anxiety by concentrating on the exhilarating feeling of being free, by losing herself in the beauty of her surroundings.

Grant Hunter paced the deck of his oil rig, staring out at the gulf. The salty sea breeze whipped a lock of his brown hair onto his forehead. He was preoccupied, oblivious to the rumbling of the engines and generators that kept the huge structure operating.

Why was he so disturbed this evening? The answer was obvious. *Leida Adams.*

She had come suddenly into his life and was proving to be profoundly disconcerting. Was it because of the mystery about her? No, he was sure it went deeper than that. Something about her had touched him. She was causing him to take an uncomfortable inventory of his life. Why? He struggled with that question. Was it because Leida reminded him of that other time in his life, the turbulent period when he'd severed relations with his family and had struck out on his own?

Half-forgotten memories jumbled through his mind—the tramp steamers, the backbreaking work, the distant ports, the foreign tongues, the acid taste of fear in his mouth and the moments of exultation when he knew he'd met life on his own terms and hadn't backed down.

They were memories he savored; his own personal drama that he'd once lived. At times, now that he was burdened with pressures and responsibilities, it all seemed very distant, like a fascinating novel he'd once read. But back then, he'd played the main part in the adventure. He'd been alive and vital and life had been sweet.

Now a quirk of fate had brought a woman into his life who somehow returned him to those times. Somehow, in a way he couldn't analyze—a way that was almost mystical—she had caused him to recapture that younger, more vital image of himself. Being with her today had brought back that sense of aliveness, of excitement, of adventure.

He tried to get a grip on that. What was it about Leida that had awakened those feelings in him? He considered himself an excellent judge of human nature. His experience as a trial lawyer had helped equip him with that ability. He had developed a sixth sense about human nature—a talent that stood him in good stead now as a politician.

It was that ability that had given him an insight into Leida Adams in the short time they had been together. He sized her up as a feisty woman whose strength of character was striking. Somehow, somewhere, that young woman had battled with life. As yet, he didn't know any of the details. But he saw in her eyes that the stakes must have been high. He saw an old sadness tinged with bitterness, but also an unquenchable strength. In her own words, she was a survivor. The combination made her irresistibly fascinating.

Yes, he concluded, it was those qualities that had made such an impact on him. The direction his life was taking these days was making him feel boxed in. Lately, he had felt a loss of control over his life as political pressures, his campaign manager, his father, even Alice, his fiancée, had taken charge of his time. Perhaps he felt some of the old rebellion stirring.

That made Leida enormously appealing. It somehow added fuel to her physical attractiveness.

Dangerous fantasies were creeping into his imagination, seductive visions of Leida's full lips, the hollow of her throat, the aura of scented fragrance that surrounded her, emphasizing her femininity. The tempting fantasies slowly opened the buttons of her blouse, one by one, until it fell away from the creamy secrets it had hidden—and his blood throbbed.

Dangerous fantasies for a man engaged to another woman....

"Thanks, Jim," Leida said. She took the strong, tattooed arm of Jim Marshall, her weekend neighbor. He helped Leida from her sailboat onto one of the piers that jutted out from the shore.

This secluded cove was where Leida spent her weekends in her rented houseboat. It was a tiny community and the people who lived here were a friendly lot who preferred the waterfront tranquillity to the pressures of urban civilization.

"Thank goodness you're all right, Leida," Jim said around the stump of a pipe clenched between his teeth.

"We were all worried about you. We weren't sure whether you'd gone back to Austin early or if you were caught out in that gulf storm that blew up so suddenly. Your car was still here, but you've had trouble with it before and had to take the bus back. When we couldn't locate your boat, we searched to see if it'd broken loose from its moorings. We notified the Coast Guard, but we didn't hear anything. Next time, let somebody know when you're going to be gone overnight in your sailboat."

"Sure, Jim." Leida nodded. She hesitated about telling him what had happened. She didn't want to talk about her experience. The residents of the little waterfront community would find out soon enough. The media would be spreading the story about her near drowning and rescue on tonight's TV news. Leida felt sure her photograph would be splashed across the front of tomorrow's newspapers.

She got angry when she thought about how friendly and pleased Senator Grant Hunter had appeared when the reporters and TV people had cornered them. She was almost certain he had tipped off the media. Getting all that publicity about being a hero wasn't going to hurt his political image a bit!

Jim's wife, Dora, a short thin woman with graying hair, hurried out onto the pier. "Leida," she called happily. "You're a sight for sore eyes, honey. We've been worried about you."

"So Jim said," Leida replied, smiling.

"It's late and you look tired. I've got a pot of seafood gumbo cooking. Have supper with us and tell us what you've been up to. Did you find a new place to paint?''

Leida sighed. "Thanks, Dora. I really appreciate the offer. But I'm a little tired. I think I'll just stay at my place, have a sandwich and go to bed early. Okay?'' She didn't want to hurt their feelings. They were two of her closest friends on the waterfront. They'd lived here for several years. They'd wanted to escape the icy northern winters and the snow after Jim's retirement. Life here was simple.

That was one of the reasons Leida enjoyed her weekend retreats. Time seemed to slow down and the relaxed atmosphere stimulated her desire to paint. She'd captured many of the scenes so familiar to the waterfront—the fishing boats with their riot of shrimp nets spreading out like fans from the mast, fishermen with their catch of redfish and trout, little children sharing time with grandfathers on the edge of the water while waiting for a bite on their fishing line.

One scene she especially loved was a picture she'd painted of a mother and daughter walking hand-in-hand to the water's edge, their forms silhouetted against a golden orange sunset.

"Okay, honey," Dora said, nodding. "But you know we have plenty if you change your mind."

"Thanks," she said, patting her friend on the arm.

She chatted with Dora and Jim as she headed for her place, waving to several other friends as she passed by. The community was populated with a wide assortment of people ranging from a former schoolteacher to an ex-pilot. One of the boat people was a poet. Another was a computer hacker who lived in a ramshackle shrimp boat converted to permanent living quarters. He kept in touch with local and national networks through a computer modem hooked up to a telephone line that was strung to his boat.

Most of the residents had discovered this place by accident when they were fishing or were passing through on their way somewhere else. They'd stayed for a while and then had decided they liked the uncomplicated, unhurried pace of life. All the dwellings were small, simple, but adequate.

Leida liked the camaraderie of the community. Once an outsider was accepted, the group stuck together like a close-knit family. Leida never locked the door of her houseboat. She never worried that her sailboat might be stolen. There were ears and eyes everywhere looking out for her welfare.

Once on board her houseboat, Leida turned on the lights. The walls were covered with her colorful paintings and with various beachcombing treasures—glass fishing floats, seashells, fishing nets, oddly shaped bits of driftwood. After glancing around, she sank wearily onto the couch, ready to admit that she was tired. The gentle rocking of her home on the water was like being cradled as a child. It was a soothing sensation.

A good night's sleep should return her to normal, she thought, stretching out on the couch and closing her eyes. Immediately the face of Grant Hunter popped into her mind. With it came a surge of conflicting, disturbing emotions.

"Oh, no, you don't," she muttered. She bolted upright and grabbed for a sketch pad and pencil she always kept on the stand nearby. Quickly she sketched his face, only this time it was not a caricature. She paused over the portrait, forgetting about the time, filling in little details that brought character to the simple line drawing. She worked skillfully, recalling how kind he'd been to her, and the kindness showed up in the softness of the lines around his mouth. She remembered how strong he was, and she drew his firm chin and determined jawline.

She worked for a long time. Finally she put down her pencil and sighed. "There," she said, holding up her sketch. "Now I have you out of my system, Grant Hunter. You're just a drawing on a sketch pad. Putting you down on paper has robbed you of your mystique. Now I know all about you, and I find you utterly ordinary. Utterly."

She tossed the sketch pad on the table and stood up. She stretched and took a deep breath. Until this minute she hadn't realized how hungry she felt. She traversed the worn carpet of the living area and rummaged in the cabinets for something to eat. The interior of her houseboat was like the inside of a small trailer. All the necessities were there, but it was small and open, except for the bedroom, which was separate from the rest.

Leida saw no point in buying quantities of groceries for her weekend trips, so she usually kept canned goods and boxed foods here on the coast. She found a jar of crunchy peanut butter, made a sandwich and opened a bottle of cola, then left the small kitchen and returned to the living room area. She had her choice of the couch or one chair to sit on.

She flopped on the couch and bit into the sandwich. As she did so her gaze flitted across Grant Hunter's portrait. Her attention was arrested. She bit her bottom lip. "Look," she said, irritated. "I owe you my life. You saved me from drowning, okay? But what right do you have to invade my privacy like this? You got paid back with all the publicity you're going to get. I think you engineered that little impromptu press conference at the boat shop." She put down her sandwich, picked up the sketch and stared at it for a moment. Then she tossed the pad back on the table facedown. "There, that ought to take care of you," she muttered.

She finished her sandwich, downed her drink and noticed the clock on the wall. It was news time. Well, she thought miserably, she might as well turn on the TV and find out just how extensive the local coverage of Grant's heroics would be.

Grant Hunter flopped on one of the bunk beds on the *Hacienda* oil rig. He entwined his fingers and put them behind his head, resting the back of his head on his palms. As he stared off into space thoughtfully, he wondered if Leida had watched the evening news before going to bed. If so, what was her reaction to the coverage the rescue had been given? He'd gotten the impression she didn't like that kind of publicity. Why? What was her reason for becoming so upset over the media? What was she hiding from?

The TV cameras had shown the two of them emerging from the boat shop, and then coverage of the brief interview. The rescue was big news, and a close-up of

Leida's face had been splashed across the screen. She was simply identified as Leida Adams, a local artist.

Grant was portrayed as a hero who dived into the black waters of the gulf at midnight to rescue her. That kind of sensationalism embarrassed him and made him uncomfortable, but his campaign manager would no doubt love it. Grant would have much preferred to keep the whole incident quiet, but he had to cooperate with the media.

He remembered that Leida had been strangely withdrawn, almost angry after their confrontation with the press. Why? What was the real story about Leida Adams? Who was she? He had to find out more about her.

The next morning, Leida strode briskly into the newspaper office building. Physically, she felt fully recovered from her ordeal on the gulf. But emotionally she was shattered. She'd been awake most of the night; it was impossible to relax enough to fall asleep after seeing her image splashed across the TV screen.

She didn't like calling attention to herself, especially not on the state level. She'd agreed to the political cartooning job on the condition that she not be identified in the press. She didn't want anyone recognizing her and perhaps connecting her with the past she'd worked so hard to leave behind.

It had been a wrenching experience to leave her hometown when she did, but her life there had taken an ugly turn. She'd stayed and fought it as long as she could. Finally she'd realized the hopelessness of the situation. In despair, she'd left and set out to make a new life for herself.

She'd tried to forget about the past, but the story of her rescue printed in newspapers across the state made her realize how fragile her new identity was.

Would someone recognize her and identify her as Leida Wilson?

Her real name... Leida Wilson. What a torrent of wrenching memories it evoked!

She thought about her twin sister, Kara, and how close they had been. Leida shivered, remembering how often it had felt as if it was the two of them against the world. Leida and Kara had shared the cruel antagonism of their clannish little East Texas hometown, the stigma of their family's reputation and the sordid home environment.

Their home was tacked onto the back of a bar run by their father, Jim Wilson, a belligerent, hard-drinking man. Leida could remember going to sleep every night to the sounds of the jukebox playing loud country and western songs and of the noisy voices of the rowdy, brawling crowd.

Their older brother, Jeff, had been in trouble all his life, stealing, fighting, racing through the streets in a souped-up jalopy. The whole community breathed a sigh of relief when he finally left town.

When Leida remembered her home life, her mother seemed to fade into the shadows. Much stronger was the image of her aunt, Maizy. Aunt Maizy was a tall, red-haired woman with a brassy voice and piercing blue eyes. She helped run the bar owned by her brother, the girls' father. She was the one person in town who wasn't afraid of Jim Wilson. Leida doubted if Aunt Maizy was afraid of the devil himself.

With all her loud, brassy ways, Maizy was a pussycat where the twins were concerned. Her gruff exterior didn't fool Leida and Kara one bit; they knew Maizy had a big heart. It was Maizy who gave Leida the courage to face the cruel gossip and prejudice of the town. "Lift your chin and look 'em right in the eye, honey," Maizy counseled. "You're as good as any of 'em and better'n most of them snooty people." Later, it was Maizy who advised Leida to shake the dust of the town from her feet and start a new life someplace else. Leida would be eternally grateful for that.

Their home on the wrong side of the tracks and the reputation of their father and brother had spilled over into her and Kara's lives, setting the town gossips against them. Before they were out of elementary school they were known scornfully as "those Wilson girls." They never had a chance. The more respectable families had already labeled them as undesirable trash.

The resemblance between Leida and Kara was incredible. When they dressed alike and wore the same hairstyles, few townsfolk could tell them apart. They seized on the uncanny resemblance as both a defense and a way of playfully tweaking the noses of the self-righteous gossips.

At school, they played tricks on teachers, taking each other's classes. When they began dating, more than once a boy thought he was taking out Leida when it was actually Kara with whom he spent the evening.

Leida recalled one evening in particular when she and Kara had double-dated. So their dates could tell them apart, Kara wore a fake beauty spot on her left cheek. Afterward, they sat on their twin beds, laughing over the events of the evening.

"It was a riot!" Kara giggled, tears of laughter welling up in her eyes. Her curly, dark hair framed her animated face.

During the evening, they had gone to the rest room together and switched the beauty spot. They changed identities several times without their dates ever suspecting.

The old, bittersweet memories brought a wrench of pain. Resolutely, Leida put them aside. She didn't have time to think about the past now. She'd been away from the newspaper for several days and wondered how much material would be stacked on her desk. In addition to her Alex Carter political cartoons, she still did artwork for feature articles.

Leida nodded at the security guard at the main entrance. He smiled, then strode over to her.

"Hi, Miss Adams," he said lightly. "I wondered where you'd been the past couple of days. I see by the morning paper you almost drowned. Sure glad you're okay."

Leida froze. A sinking feeling plummeted from her head to her toes. "Morning, George," she said faintly.

She gathered her courage and took the elevator to the newsroom.

Chapter Five

So this is why you were so noncommittal on the phone about what had happened." Sam Daniels, Leida's editor, chuckled. His blue eyes sparkled. He tossed the morning paper in front of Leida.

Seated on the other side of the large oak desk in Sam's meticulous office, Leida glanced down at the now familiar photograph and pressed her lips together in an angry line.

Sam, a man in his early sixties with thinning gray hair and a slender frame, cast an amused look in her direction. "Well, well, Alex Carter, alias Leida Adams, alias the Mystery Woman who shuns the press. It seems the mystery was cleared up by someone in your coastal community who identified you as a local artist living on a houseboat."

"At least they didn't trace me any further than that," she muttered.

Sam, still grinning, said, "I can see the story now. Senator Hunter rescues Leida Adams who turns out to be Alex Carter, the famous cartoonist—and Hunter's political enemy. He then throws her back to the sharks."

"You have a warped sense of humor, Sam," Leida retorted.

"It would make a great story. I have half a mind to release it."

"You wouldn't dare!" she gasped. "You gave me your word you'd keep me anonymous if I drew those cartoons. Sam, if you print that story, I'll quit. I'll never draw another Alex Carter cartoon!"

The editor held up both hands in mock surrender. "Only teasing. Except for myself and a couple of political writers for the editorial page, nobody knows the identity of Alex Carter and it will stay that way. You're right. I gave you my word and I'll keep it." Then he asked, "How does it feel to have been rescued by the man you've been lambasting with your cartoons for the past six months?"

Leida frowned. "There hasn't been anything personal in my caricatures. I was just getting across a political idea."

Sam laughed. "Come off it, Leida. Everyone admires the venom in your pen. You make Hunter look like a monster. Your caricatures are fantastic. They emphasize the hidden, dark side of Hunter's character. You, of all people, should realize how ruthless the man is. Look what he's done with the story of your rescue. It was a stroke of genius. Call out the press, play up the hero image. I couldn't have thought of a better media strategy myself."

"Yeah." Leida sighed, a feeling of bitter disillusionment sweeping over her. "I guess that showed his true character, all right."

"You certainly didn't expect anything less from a politician like Hunter, did you?" Sam asked. "You know how the game is played."

Yes, she had expected more from Grant than to use her to further his own ambitions. He'd treated her so well, had been so kind and solicitous to her. She had begun to think he was a real gentleman. Now she realized she had been a fool to take his actions and manner personally. He was, after all, an unfeeling political animal, just as her newspaper had been characterizing him all along!

"Sure," she said in a monotone. "I know how the game is played. I've characterized enough of it for you on the editorial page, haven't I?"

"Yes, and you've done a marvelous job. Now, let me tell you what I have in mind for our next series of cartoons. We'll ease up on him a bit for a couple of weeks until this hero stuff blows over, then we'll hit him with both barrels...."

Leida was listening to Sam with that half of her brain that processed the factual information she dealt with on her job. But the emotional side of her mind had tuned him out and was stewing over Grant Hunter. She was itching to draw him again. If he thought Alex Carter had made him ugly before, just wait until she got through with him now!

It was the following weekend.

Leida pulled her sailboat up to the dock behind Grant Hunter's house. She was determined to repay him for her sail, and then she never wanted to see him again.

It was a hot, blistering summer day. Even the cooling breeze off the gulf couldn't smooth off the sharp edge of her ire toward Grant Hunter for using her to enhance his image.

She jumped on the dock from her boat and trotted rapidly down the pier toward the beach. Her jogging shoes made grids in the sand as she marched toward his beach house. The closer she got to Grant Hunter, the hotter and angrier she became. However, she was determined not to let him see how irritated she really was. She would be cool and businesslike when she reimbursed him for the sail. As for her personal feelings, she could give vent to them in her cartoons.

She climbed the steps to the front door and held her breath as she rapped. She heard nothing. She knocked again. Total silence. She waited. Then she turned and descended the steps, checking under the house where Grant had parked his car. The space was empty. The house was deserted. Even the housekeeper, Mrs. Garcia, was absent. So, he hadn't come to the beach this weekend.

She felt a strange letdown feeling. She had come here to repay him for the sail. Was there some other reason she'd looked forward to seeing him again? She instantly recoiled at the thought. Absolutely not!

Leida left. But she'd be back the next weekend. She was determined not to remain in debt to Hunter. As far as she was concerned it was a debt of honor, a matter of pride. She had no intention of allowing a man she despised to pay for her sail.

It was true, he had saved her life. For that she was grateful. But he needn't have used the incident for his own gain. If he wanted her to issue a statement to the press, common decency dictated that he at least ask her how she felt about it before he unleashed those reporters on her when she least expected it.

The next week at the newspaper was a busy one for Leida. By week's end she was ready for her usual trip to the coast to enjoy the leisurely pace of life on her houseboat. While there she would try again to pay Grant Hunter the money she owed him.

On Saturday afternoon, Leida arrived in her sailboat at Grant's beach house. She pulled up to the dock as before and tied her boat securely. There were several starfish and sand dollars washed upon the shore. She stopped to look at them. Nearby lay a purplish-blue, inflated, balloonlike object. It was a Portuguese man-of-war jellyfish, a beautiful but treacherous type of sea creature with venom capable of inflicting agonizing stings and leaving permanent scars. It reminded her of Grant Hunter.

Instantly Leida painted the scene in her mind. There was such a contrast between the beautiful innocent shellfish and the even more beautiful but deadly man-of-war. When she got back to her houseboat, she would paint the tableau just as she was now seeing it.

She walked down the pier and toward the house. It wasn't until she drew closer that she saw several cars parked near the front. People dressed in casual but expensive-looking clothes were climbing into sleek automobiles, waving and laughing, and pulling out of the yard.

Suddenly, Leida felt embarrassed. It had been so quiet when she was here before. It hadn't occurred to her that a party might be going on. She certainly wasn't going to intrude.

She stopped and was about to turn around. Just then the door opened and Grant appeared. Leida froze to the spot, the sight of him taking her breath away.

"Leida!" he exclaimed. "You came back!" He strode swiftly across the hard-packed sand toward her. He wore an open-throated tan shirt and dark trousers. The sun glinted on his brown hair, giving it a burnished look.

Leida gained her composure, raising her chin, her gaze cool.

Coming up to her, he grasped both her hands before she could avoid him. The sudden contact made her feel strangely weak. "Why did you leave that afternoon without saying goodbye?" he asked accusingly. "You promised you'd wait until I returned. I was concerned about you. You weren't ready to sail off by yourself."

"I changed my mind. I did just fine," she said coolly. "I only came to pay you for my sail."

He stood looking down at her with a perplexed expression. Then he said, "You don't have to pay me for the sail."

"I told you I wouldn't take it unless you allowed me to repay you!" He might have no integrity, but she darn sure did. She thrust her hand in the pocket of her white pedal pushers and pulled out the cash she'd brought along. "I pay my debts," she retorted.

Grant looked at her for a long moment, as if trying to understand the hostility in her eyes. "Okay," he said slowly, "I can see it's important to you. You have a lot of pride, don't you?"

She thrust the roll of bills into his hand without replying.

Grant didn't count it.

"It's all there," she said.

"I'm sure it is, Leida," he said. "I could tell from the first time we met that you're a young woman with a lot of character."

She looked up at him and bit her lip. Darn him! She wanted to tell him off, to really let him have it. She had her speech memorized, ready to berate him for the ruthless, political maneuver of making himself into a hero for the press. Now he'd blasted a hole in her frontal assault with a sincere compliment, telling her she had character!

For a moment, her composure was demolished. A wave of old, hurting memories was awakened. Character. That was the last thing the people in her hometown would have said about "those Wilson girls."

Grant had touched a vulnerable spot. He seemed adept at that—as if he had a sixth sense and knew where she was most defenseless.

"Why—why did you say that?" she stammered.

"What? That you have character?" He looked puzzled. "Because you do. Anybody who's around you five minutes can see it."

"Really?" she asked, unconvinced.

"Certainly. I'm sure you know that."

For a moment, Leida felt a stab of guilt over all the mean things she'd been thinking about him. Then she got angry all over again. "Darn you, Grant Hunter!" she exclaimed. "I came here to tell you to your face what I think of you."

He looked surprised and a bit angry himself. "I don't understand. What do you mean? I can tell you're upset about something. What did I do?"

"What did you do?" she gasped. "You know exactly what I mean. You deliberately set the media on us at the boat shop so you could play up your image. You saw a chance to get some good publicity and you tipped off the media. I don't appreciate being used to get you votes!"

For a moment Grant appeared speechless by her outburst. Then his jaw knotted and an angry flame kindled in his eyes. Leida took a step backward. She had never seen his anger stirred up before. As big as he was, she suddenly thought, he could be a very dangerous man if aroused. Had she pushed him too far? Her knees suddenly felt a bit weak. She wondered if they would support her if she turned and ran.

But then the flash of anger faded from his eyes. In its place came amusement. He threw back his head and laughed. It was a hearty, robust laugh that dissolved her momentary uneasiness.

"Leida." Grant took her hand in his and patted it. His brown eyes were filled now with that special warmth that could engulf her like a tender caress. "I can't blame you for being upset with me, if that's what you believe. And I can see how you could jump to that kind of conclusion. Leida, I swear I didn't call the media about the rescue. Heaven knows I need all the favorable publicity I can get, but I certainly wouldn't use your almost drowning to drum up sympathy. Believe me, the reporters called the house after we'd left. Mrs. Garcia told them where we'd gone. I had no idea the story had even been spread around town. Probably one of the rig operators talked about it. I was as surprised as you were when the reporters showed up."

Leida looked at her hand in Grant's. She wanted to retrieve it. But she wanted more not to. She also wanted to believe him, but a residue of doubt lingered. "You were awfully nice to those reporters. You didn't act the least bit upset."

"I have to be agreeable to the press, Leida. It's one of the burdens of running for public office. I've had a lot of practice over the years dealing with the media. Even a rebuff has to be handled diplomatically."

"I'm not sure I believe you," she said defensively.

"If I wanted to use you for publicity, do you think I'd have whisked you away from there as soon as I saw how distressed you were about the situation? I could have let the interview proceed."

She had to admit that was true. Now he had her confused again. Leida became disturbingly aware that Grant was still holding her hand. The physical contact was arousing emotions that were unsettling. She withdrew her hand.

"I'd like to believe you."

"I wish you would," he said, looking deeply into her eyes.

Suddenly she recalled trying to convince a skeptical teacher that she and Kara hadn't cheated on a test. They were innocent. But the teacher had chosen to believe their reputation rather than the girls' claim of innocence. It had been awful to be wrongfully accused.

Was Leida doing the same thing to Grant, believing the reputation rather than the man? Was she doing him an injustice? Or was he the type that could make her believe anything?

"Well," she said crisply, "I guess it really doesn't matter what I believe. I've accomplished what I came for. I better be going." She turned to leave. Grant's fingers curled around her wrist and stopped her.

"It matters to me," he said softly.

He stood so close to her she could hear him breathing. She swallowed hard. It was wrong of her to think ill of him when she had no proof. She ducked her head slightly. "I'm sorry," she said contritely. "I had no right to jump to conclusions." She looked at him.

He smiled. "It's all right," he said in a cheerful voice. "I'd probably have thought the same thing."

They looked at each other for an electric instant and she could feel an almost tangible current pass between them. Leida wasn't sure what it was, but it jolted her and she could see by Grant's eyes that he'd felt it, too. Her cheeks grew warm as she gingerly twisted her wrist from Grant's grasp. He released her slowly.

"I better go," she repeated and looked away.

"Not so fast," Grant countered. "I never did get to show you the other side of those trees you were interested in painting, remember?"

"Thanks, but you have company."

"Not anymore. The party just ended. I'm free for the rest of the afternoon."

"I have to finish a canvas I started this morning." She hoped she sounded sufficiently breezy. "Maybe some other time."

"But there is something I want to show you before you leave. It won't take a minute. Okay?"

She relented. "Okay."

"It's this way." He gestured toward his house. Leida walked beside him. Sea oats, swaying lazily in the gulf breeze, brushed their legs.

They rounded the edge of the house. Grant picked up an object and held it out for Leida's inspection. It was a beautiful piece of mauve driftwood twisted like the arms of a graceful ballerina. From its center grew a bright red flower.

"This washed up the night of the storm," Grant explained. "When I found out you were an artist, I intended giving it to you, but you got away before I had a chance even to tell you about it."

"Why, it's lovely," Leida exclaimed. She took the driftwood in her hands for closer examination. Its exterior was almost glassy smooth, as if it had been polished by the hand of a master craftsman. But she knew the finish was nature's doing, a delicate silver patina painted by the sun and wind. How the flower came to be growing in the center was a mystery. Perhaps there was a pocket of earth inside the wood.

She glanced from the driftwood to Grant. "Thank you."

"The pleasure's mine," he said, smiling. "But if you really want to thank me, how about a boat ride? I need to take my boat on a little spin to check out the engine. Why don't you come along and keep me company?"

"I don't know," she said hesitantly. "There's that canvas I started..."

"It'll keep, won't it?" Grant asked. The intensity of his brown eyes made her heart pick up tempo.

She fidgeted with the driftwood in her hands, nervously rubbing one end with her thumb. "I guess so," she admitted.

"Good!" His voice was filled with genuine warmth.

The late-afternoon sun shimmered on the choppy water. The breeze blew gently, stirring tendrils of Leida's long dark hair. She was acutely aware of Grant's gaze roaming her features, her figure. Any woman was aware of a look like that. It was the look of a man drinking in the sight of a woman he found desirable. It brought a flush of warmth to her face, her body. She could not honestly say she did not like it.

"Let's—let's go, then," she said self-consciously. He nodded and they walked to the pier where a sleek blue and white outboard motorboat was docked.

He untied his boat from its moorings, held the rope in his hand and gestured for Leida to board. As she did so, he took her by the arm and helped her in. She felt a twinge of anxiety. Perhaps for a while she would have that momentary feeling every time she got in a boat. But she relaxed as she looked at Grant. Being out on the water wouldn't be quite so unsettling with him along. She had the instinctual feeling that he could take care of her under any circumstances.

Leida took the seat next to the driver's and breathed deeply of the salty air. This was home to her. No matter that the dark sea had betrayed her and nearly swallowed her up. Part of the lure of the coast was the treacherousness of the elements. It was her own fault she'd almost drowned. She'd stupidly ignored the warning issued by nature of the impending storm. It wouldn't happen again, she felt sure of that.

Leida heard the low roar of the engine, felt the wind gently whipping around her face as the craft picked up speed. Grant headed out toward the gulf.

She watched with fascination as the boat skimmed over the surface of the water, slicing through it like a sharp knife. There was an ephemeral beauty about the water, a haunting quality that made her feel almost one with the ebb and flow of the tides.

She'd painted many waterfront scenes, but she never felt entirely satisfied with her work. There was an elusive quality she longed to depict in her paintings, a real sense of depth and purpose. If she could just capture that quality in her work, she'd feel satisfied.

Soul. That was the key word. Some people thought great artists expressed themselves so profoundly because their work mirrored suffering in their lives. Only those whose souls had been profoundly wrenched were capable of great artistry.

Leida wasn't sure that was true, but if it were, she should be capable of capturing that elusive quality in her work. She recalled Kara. It always hurt to remember her twin sister, but not to think about her would be like pretending Kara had never existed.

Soul. Yes, Leida understood the word well. Only one who'd grown up with an identical twin could understand the inseparable bond between such sisters. They were so much alike and yet, in the final analysis, so different. There was a bittersweet poignancy in recalling Kara, of mentally reliving their relationship before the tragedy.

Suddenly Leida was shaken from her reverie, realizing Grant had spoken to her. "What?" Leida asked.

"I wondered if you were nervous."

She shook her head and smiled. "No. I'm sorry. I was just enjoying the scenery."

"I sensed you were doing more than enjoying it," Grant observed. "You seemed lost in it. I thought maybe you were recalling the accident."

"That was the farthest thing from my mind," she said lightly. "I was thinking about the view. I love the water, the sky, the meeting of the two, like two lost lovers forced apart who finally come together and join hands for all eternity where they meet on the horizon."

"That sounds poetic. Do you write poetry in addition to painting?"

She chuckled. "No. I'm afraid not."

There was a pause. Grant looked back at the water, over at her thoughtfully, and then spoke. "Tell me about your painting. I sense it's very important to you."

She shrugged. "It's what I like most to do."

"I'd like to see some of your work."

Suddenly Leida felt defensive. "If I ever have a gallery showing, maybe you will."

"You mean I have to wait for an art show?"

Leida hesitated. Obviously, he was asking for an invitation to her place. But how could she allow him to find out anything about her? "I don't have anything ready for anyone to see, yet," she hedged. "I'm working on a series of paintings now."

"Scenes along the coastline?"

"Yes."

"That's why you wanted to stop and examine the tree we passed on the way into town."

"Yes. But after all the commotion at the boat shop, I wouldn't have been in any frame of mind to appreciate its beauty."

"Maybe I can show it to you another time," he suggested.

"Yes."

"How about next week?" he asked.

"I can't make any plans just yet," she said. "Thanks anyway." Leida looked away and then down at her hands. This conversation was becoming uncomfortable.

Grant stared out at the water in front of him for a moment, guiding the boat. "I have the feeling that you're going to disappear any minute," he said solemnly.

Leida felt a twinge of remorse. He'd hit so close to home. She wanted to disappear. But she wasn't about to let him know that. "That's because the gulf is so beautiful," she said. "It stretches out endlessly, as if one could disappear into its beauty, absorbed by its

strength and majesty." That wasn't what he'd meant
and she knew it.

Grant was silent for a moment. Then he pointed in
the direction of a tiny figure on the horizon. "There's
the oil rig," he said.

Leida gasped. It was so far from land. She was
shocked at how far she'd been dragged out to sea. "I
had no idea..." she murmured, her voice trailing off.
She felt a little queasy.

"Do you want to go back?" Grant asked, giving her
a concerned look.

"Yes, if you don't mind," Leida replied. "It's not
the oil rig. But I need to get back. Has your engine
checked out okay?"

Grant nodded. "Yes, it's fine."

Had there really been anything to check out on it?
Leida wondered. He steered the motorboat in a wide
arc and headed back toward land.

The sun's rays, which until now had been behind
them, were now reflected off the water and almost
blinded them. Grant opened the glove compartment
and took out two pairs of sunglasses, one for him and
one for her.

"Thanks," she said, putting them on.

Grant nodded silently. She could think of nothing
to say. She felt awkward.

Finally Grant spoke. "Leida, I'm about to return
you to shore, and I still don't know anything about
you. I don't know why you're such a private person.
But I've half a mind to kidnap you and hold you hos-
tage on my oil rig if you don't tell me something more

specific about yourself. All I know is that you live in that little waterfront community a few miles down the coast and that you're an artist. What are you trying to hide?''

Chapter Six

Hide?'' Leida looked at him sharply. "What makes you think I have anything to hide?''

He pulled off his sunglasses and returned her look, his brown-eyed gaze penetrating. He called her bluff. "Do you?''

She turned away, her gaze flitting to the dusky blue water with its gentle whitecaps. For a moment, the vision of the caricatures she had drawn of him flashed across her mind and she felt a stab of guilt. Then an unreasonable anger swelled up in her like the surging of the evening tide. What right did he have to pry into her private affairs, anyway? He'd saved her from drowning, and for that she was grateful. An accident of fate had brought them together. But she wasn't obligated to tell him the story of her life!

If she told him the truth, that she was Alex Carter, the political cartoonist who was such a thorn in his side, there could be only one result: the warm feeling between them would turn into bitterness and hate. She didn't want that. She'd rather go on playing the masquerade. After today she probably wouldn't ever see him again anyway.

"Everybody has something to hide," she tossed back lightly. "There's a skeleton in every family closet."

Grant's searching stare wouldn't relent. "What skeleton is hiding in your closet, Leida Adams?"

She shrugged and kept her tone light. "None of your business, Senator Hunter."

"Please, don't start that 'Senator Hunter' stuff again."

"All right, Grant," she agreed, reluctantly, sensing the loss of another defense against a growing familiarity with this intriguing man.

"Back to the skeleton matter. Your skeleton wouldn't by any chance be a husband you haven't told me about?"

This time her laugh was genuine. "Certainly not!"

He looked relieved. "Well, I'm glad to hear that!"

Before he could pursue the matter further, a motorboat suddenly pulled up alongside them. Leida saw that it bore the emblem of the United States as well as the shield of the Coast Guard. Two men in crisp white uniforms waved and smiled. Grant pulled back on the throttle of the boat and slowed to a stop.

"Sorry to bother you, sir," one of the men said, "but we're checking boats in the area today. May I see your registration papers, please?"

Grant nodded affably and removed a plastic bag containing papers from the glove compartment. He stood and handed it to the officer.

The officer glanced at the papers and said, "Oh, Senator Hunter. I'm sorry. I didn't recognize you." He returned the papers. "I'm sure everything is fine. If you'll just show me your life preservers, fire extinguisher and flares, sir, I'll be on my way."

"Certainly," Grant responded.

The two men made a quick check of the items required by law, gave a parting salute and sped away.

Leida sighed. Saved by the law. The inspection gave her a moment to gather her wits. She was determined to steer the conversation in a new direction.

Leida remembered the piece of driftwood Grant had given her. She'd brought it along on the boat ride, placing it on the seat beside her. Now she picked it up.

"I'm really looking forward to painting this," she said. "Thank you for giving it to me."

The subject of Leida's identity was closed. She'd slammed the door on any further discussion in that realm. Grant apparently became resigned to her stubborn clinging to her privacy. He didn't bring up the matter again. He put the boat in gear and headed toward land.

Back at the pier he helped her out of the boat.

She walked across the pier to her sailboat, where she knelt and carefully placed the piece of driftwood in her boat. Grant followed her. "Am I going to see you again?"

Leida removed her sunglasses and placed them in his hand. "Thanks for the ride," she said lightly. "I'm sure we'll see each other around sometime."

"Sometime?" he asked. He placed the glasses in his shirt pocket and took her hands in his as if reluctant to let her leave.

Leida felt a growing panic. She was afraid of what would happen if she stayed any longer—she had to get away. But Grant was intent on finding some reason to keep her there.

He studied her hands, then gently ran his fingers over hers. Tiny shock waves raced up her arms, sending a shiver through her body. What kind of insanity is this? she wondered. It was sheer madness to allow herself to become attracted to this man, to feel a throbbing heat at his touch, a weak trembling in her knees at his eye contact. She was on a collision course with disaster!

Her thoughts whirled with questions. What was happening to her? Why did he hold her hand with such tenderness; why did his eyes search her with such burning intensity? Why was he so persistent? Senator Grant Hunter was one of the most fascinating, attractive men in Texas. He was engaged to a gorgeous Texas beauty who lived in the same world as he did— a world populated by oil- and cattle-rich families who controlled the economy and politics of the state. Why would a man like Grant Hunter become interested in a little nobody he picked out of the gulf one stormy night . . . a woman he knew nothing about beyond her name?

That must be it, she thought. It was because he knew nothing about her that he was so interested. She had become a mystery that he had to solve.

But if he solved the mystery he wouldn't like what he found out! she thought with a twinge of wry irony.

Grant's voice interrupted her thoughts, "Are you going to let me see the painting of the driftwood after you've finished it?"

Leida bit her lip. "Why don't I send the painting to you?" she said. "It'll be yours to keep."

"I'd like that," he said. "But I'll accept it only on two conditions."

"What's that?" she asked warily.

"First, you deliver it in person. And second, you stay for dinner this evening."

A fresh wave of panic. "Well . . . I . . ."

"Come on," he said lightly, tugging her by the hand. "Mrs. Garcia is the best cook this side of Austin. You'll love what she can do with seafood delicacies."

Before she could protest, Grant was leading her off the pier and toward his house.

All the way to the house, she asked herself why she lacked the good sense to say "no!"

Grant walked into the dining room to check the table set for two. He glanced over the snow-white linen, the silver, the china and the crystal embossed with the letter *H*. The table setting was impeccable, complete with a centerpiece of fresh flowers. He nodded with satisfaction. Mrs. Garcia was an artist in such matters.

This evening, Grant felt vibrantly alive. He could feel a gathering excitement inside that bubbled like champagne through his veins. He knew it was Leida Adams who had awakened this feeling in him. She did something to him, something special. He wasn't sure quite what it was, but the feelings she stirred in him were powerful. He'd never met anyone quite like her, never had feelings like this before. She was the most intriguing woman he'd ever met.

Mixed with the pleasant glow, however, was a countercurrent of rational caution. Grant Hunter, you are skating on thin ice, it warned. Are you aware of the threat to your career, your life, all your plans that becoming involved with this woman—a woman you know absolutely nothing about—could present?

He sighed, wishing he didn't have to deal with reality. But the reality wasn't going to go away, he knew. He'd been in dangerous waters since the moment Leida had come into his life and he was sinking deeper.

Man, use your head, his reason urged. Feed her and send her on her way while you still have a little sense left. You don't need this kind of complication in your life. Think what it will do to your political career if you lose your head completely over this woman. You can just as well wave bye-bye to any chance for reelection.

Oh, to hell with reason, he thought recklessly. At least for tonight, he'd let his feelings take over. Maybe in the morning he'd wake up with some sense.

He rubbed the tension gathering at the back of his neck. "Leida Adams," he muttered, "you sure have turned my life upside down!"

When he returned to the study with before-dinner cocktails, he found Leida engrossed in a display of photographs of horses that occupied one wall.

"You said you were an amateur photographer. Did you take these pictures?"

"Yes, I did," he replied, handing her a cocktail. Their eyes met and held for an electric instant.

"They're very good," she commented, self-consciously looking away from him and at the photographs. "The horses are absolutely beautiful."

"D'you know something about horses?" He continued to look at her, his dark eyes smoldering.

"Not really. But anyone can see these are thoroughbreds," she replied, hoping her voice sounded casual.

"Most of them are," he agreed, but his mind was not on the horses. His thoughts were obsessed with Leida. Her wild, reckless beauty stirred that old sensation of adventure inside him.

"They're yours?"

He nodded, unable to keep his gaze from straying to the delicate curves of her profile. "We have them stabled on our ranch in West Texas." Then he forced his attention to the photographs of a separate group. "These are some of our quarter horses. Quarter horses, you know, are trained to work cattle. They're the ones I love to ride, especially that little palomino.

Her name is Ginger. I raised her and broke her myself."

Ginger. Grant remembered that she had been wild
and full of spirit. Leida was like that. He recalled the
look of stubborn pride in Leida's eyes when she insisted on repaying him for the sail. He'd known instantly from the set of her chin that if he'd refused to
accept the money it would have wounded her dignity.

Leida stared at the picture with a puzzled frown.
"But why in heaven's name are you sitting on her
holding a polo mallet? Is it some kind of joke?"

Grant chuckled. "I take it you've never heard of
cowboy polo."

"Cowboy polo?" she echoed blankly. "No, I guess
not. I've always thought of polo as an English gentleman's game, played in riding outfits and polished
boots. You're sitting there dressed in blue jeans and
cowboy boots."

Grant nodded, pleased that she seemed so fascinated with the picture. Was it just curiosity, or was she
attracted to him? The prospect made his blood course
more quickly through his body. "I'd just finished a
match in a six-state competition near Houston. Cowboy polo started back in the 1930s in Florida. Cow-
boys there swatted a ball around with palmetto fronds.
That evolved into a game where we use a twelve-inch
inflated rubber kickball and gallop back and forth
across a hundred-yard playing field. Tournaments
draw players from states like Texas, California, Wy-
oming, Montana, Arizona and Nebraska."

Leida listened spellbound.

"It's a pretty far cry from your gentleman polo played at country clubs," Grant continued. "It's a mixture of polo, rodeo, ice hockey, rugby and football. Just about anything goes—pushing, shoving and jockeying for position. Riders are allowed to cut each other off and collide as much as they want. You need to have a horse that's a heavy, bulldog-type cutting horse who isn't afraid to get in there and mix it up. Ginger, there, is my favorite. By thoroughbred standards, she's ugly and mean, but she has a rare spirit. She'll take me anywhere, and she'll outlast any other two horses on our ranch."

"Sounds like a rough game," Leida observed.

"It gets a little insane at times." Grant chuckled. "Most of us wear football helmets. I once saw a rider swing a mallet at the ball, miss it and clobber another rider. The guy kept right on playing. It wasn't until after the match he found out his jaw had been broken. The game is very popular, though. There are about eighty teams around the country playing cowboy polo today. You'll find all kinds of guys involved in the sport—ranchers, truck drivers, livestock salesmen, rodeo riders."

"Even a Texas senator." Leida smiled, daring to direct her gaze straight at him.

He nodded, his dark eyes becoming pools ready to swallow her up. "Yes, even a Texas senator."

Suddenly, Leida flushed. A sense of intimacy was blooming between them. Where would it lead? She felt uneasy, yet fascinated.

For a moment, she contemplated the broad-shouldered Texan at her side. He was a paradox. On the one hand, his manners were polished. He had the cosmopolitan manner of a man as much at home in Paris, Rome or London as in Austin. He was obviously well educated. She had read that he'd earned a law degree before getting into politics. The other side of him was this physical, aggressive man of action, who loved the dust of a horse corral and loved to mix it up in a rough-and-tumble redneck sport like cowboy polo. She could visualize him in a tuxedo at a Dallas country-club gathering or in Western boots and blue jeans, whooping it up at a country western dance in Bandera.

She sipped her cocktail, her thoughts occupied with Grant Hunter. Presently, the housekeeper announced dinner was ready.

The meal consisted of a tossed salad, flounder stuffed with a delicious mixture of crabmeat, baked potatoes, asparagus and a dessert of chocolate mousse.

Over cups of after-dinner coffee, Leida sighed with ecstasy. "You're right about Mrs. Garcia. That woman should be a chef at Antoine's."

Grant smiled. "Yes, she's a real artist in the kitchen." Then he suggested, "Why don't we take our coffee into the living room?"

Leida hesitated. "Just this one cup. I have to get back home before dark." *And before I fall any further under your spell,* she thought nervously. There was simply no denying the attraction she felt for Grant. She found herself stealing glances at him, wishing he'd touch her again. It was insanity.

Grant escorted her into the living room. She walked over to the large window with its view of the gulf beach, gazing for a moment at the beauty.

"How's the light there for painting?" Grant asked.

He was right behind her. She could almost feel the heat of his body. Then his hands touched her arms. She thought she'd melt inside. The contact was like turning on an electric current all over her body. She closed her eyes, struggling with her breath. A wave of blind, primitive desire flashed through her, ignited by his mere touch. My Lord, she thought weakly, if he asked me to go to bed with him right now I think I'd say yes. I must be losing my mind.

She grappled for sanity. "The light? Oh, it's perfect."

His hand slid down her arms caressingly.

Stop it, she thought desperately. You're seducing me and you probably don't even know it. Then she turned and saw the smoky haze in his brown eyes and she thought, yes, you do know it, you damn, irresistible scoundrel!

No! she thought furiously. He's engaged. This is going to turn into a one-night fling, and I'm not going to let that happen. I'm not going to become what everyone back home thought I was. And I'm not going to become just another conquest for Senator Grant Hunter!

Resolutely, she drew away from him, strode toward the couch, then thought better of it and took a chair instead. It was safer. He couldn't join her there.

He followed slowly and sat on the couch, facing her. For a moment the tension in the room was almost unbearable. Then he put his coffee cup on a table beside the couch. "Tell me how you became an artist," he said.

She felt a wave of relief, on safer ground now. The moment of insanity had passed.

"Well," she said, clearing her throat, "I always loved to draw, even as a young child. My grade-school teacher thought I had a born talent. I spent my time drawing and painting when I should have been doing my homework."

There was no explaining to another person about the heights to which art took one's thoughts. When Leida was painting, she became all absorbed in her work. Art had been her escape from a troubled life. That was one reason she loved it so much.

She recalled how much she and Kara had shared their love of drawing. In her mind, she could almost see the hundreds of drawings of Tony Kara had sketched. Tony was Kara's first serious love. He'd lived in a nearby small town. Kara was so enamored of him that her schoolwork suffered. She mooned over Tony day and night and spent hours drawing his portrait. His likeness appeared on her schoolbook covers, her lunch napkin, her notebook and on sheets of plain white paper she hung all over the bedroom.

It had hurt Leida almost as much as Kara when Tony suddenly dumped Kara for another girl. His mother had found out about "those Wilson girls" and poisoned the boy's mind against Kara.

Kara was crushed. She'd run into their bedroom crying, flinging herself across the bed with a torrent of sobs. Then she'd snatched all the portraits of Tony from the walls. In a fit of rage and humiliation, she'd burned them, weeping miserably as they turned to gray ashes.

After that, a red-eyed Kara had stayed up all night, feverishly drawing anything and everything. It was her escape from a broken heart, the only way she knew to dull the pain of rejection.

With an effort, Leida shook off the memories. She took a sip of coffee and went on. "I worked to put myself through art school. I thought about becoming a commercial artist, but I want to paint what appeals to me. I've illustrated a couple of children's books and I've sold a few paintings. Nothing spectacular, but enough to encourage me. What I really want is to have my own show in an art gallery. But it takes time."

"And in the meantime?" Grant asked.

Leida shrugged. "In the meantime, I have to make a living."

"With your artwork?"

She suddenly realized what he was doing, trying to gently pry a bit of information out of her about her personal life. Very devious!

"Oh," Leida said abruptly, glancing at her watch. "I do hate to run, but I must be going. Just look at the time." She jumped up from the couch and moved toward the door. Grant followed.

She turned. "Thank Mrs. Garcia for the delicious dinner," she said. "You've been more than kind."

"You've made it an evening I won't forget," Grant said. His voice grew thicker. "I mean that."

Leida swallowed past a knot in her throat.

Grant put his hands on her shoulders and pulled her close to him, his gaze piercing into hers. Her breath caught.

"Leida," he said, "I can't let you disappear without finding out more about you. I don't know why you insist on being so mysterious, but you can't hide who you are and what you are forever. Somehow...someday, I'm going to solve the mystery of Leida Adams."

"What's the matter, Leida?" Sam Daniels asked, tossing her latest cartoon of Grant Hunter on the desk. Leida picked up her work and stared at it. The drawing showed Grant towering over his opponent with a huge stick labeled Oil Clout, while big bucks bulged from his back pocket. In the background was a longhorn steer branded with a dollar sign.

Leida shrugged. "It's what you asked for, Sam."

Sam snorted. "Leida, you know this newspaper's editorial policy about Grant Hunter. After the way he used you to grab that 'hero' publicity for himself, I'm surprised you could turn in such pap. I can't print this."

Leida's blood was running hot. "What's wrong with it?"

"What's wrong with it? Look at that caricature of Grant Hunter. Where's the lantern jaw, the grotesque mouth, the clutching hands, the evil gleam in his eyes? What's happened to you? What'd you do, fall for the guy? I could have drawn a more scathing caricature than this! You've made Hunter look like an innocent high-school boy! Redo this. I want to see some fire in your drawing. Make the thing sizzle. Now get with it. We've got a deadline. I want a new cartoon on my desk Monday morning. And this time get it right!''

Leida extracted the junk mail from the rusted box on the houseboat. She flipped through it absently, her mind still stewing over the chewing-out Sam had given her about her drawing of Grant Hunter. Had she gone soft, after all?

It was hard to be objective. When Grant had been a distant politician, it had been easy to put the kind of fire in her political drawings that Sam liked. But now Leida wasn't sure how fair the newspaper was being to Grant. Perhaps they were misjudging him. Or maybe the attack on Grant was just a way to sell newspapers. Leida wasn't sure and she felt confused over the whole matter.

"Why did I become a political cartoonist, anyway?" she fumed aloud. "Why can't I do what I want to do—forget politics and spend all my time painting?" Then she answered her own question, "Because at this point, I'd starve to death; that's why!"

Leida walked back inside the houseboat still mulling over her situation, her eyes only half seeing the mail in her hand. Suddenly, the large, uneven scrawl of a familiar handwriting caught her attention. Leida tossed the rest of the junk mail in the trash as she quickly pulled the coveted letter from the rest.

She tore open the envelope. Out slipped a letter and a small photograph of a little girl with curly dark hair and luminous blue eyes. Karen! Tears came to Leida's eyes. She sat down and quickly read the letter. Aunt

Maizy recounted Karen's first experience with swimming. The child was a natural in the water. She'd learned to paddle and go underwater during her first lesson.

Leida felt a pang for her twin sister's child. One day she wanted to have Karen live with her. But she was too mobile right now, too unsettled in her own life. She was gone all day working. Karen needed somebody like Aunt Maizy, a solid, stable woman to take care of her.

Leida looked at the photograph again and smiled. Karen was the one bright spot from her past. She was a precious child. And she looked just like Kara and Leida.

Leida wondered how Karen would react someday if she ever found out the truth about her birth. She recalled the fateful chain of events that led up to it.

Kara had been so broken up over Tony that she hardly ate for weeks. She had grown thin and pale. Leida's attempts to cheer her twin were useless.

Finally, Leida arranged a double date for the two of them. At first Kara had refused to go, but Leida insisted. Kara finally gave in.

Leida didn't notice the change in Kara's behavior right away. But after the drive-in movie, Leida was embarrassed at the way Kara and her date carried on in the back seat.

At home she flew into Kara.

"How could you act like that?" Leida demanded. "You know what people think of us already. How's it going to look when Joe spreads it around town that he was making out with you in the back seat of Butch's car?''

"He wasn't making out with me," Kara defended herself. "We were just kissing, that's all."

The argument went on until finally Kara broke down in sobs. "Oh, Leida, I'm sorry. I did act awful. But I miss Tony so much. I just can't forget him. I let Joe kiss me like that because I was feeling so miserable. He took my mind off myself. I felt good when he was holding me. It's the first time I've felt good in weeks."

Leida looked at her twin for a moment and then hugged her sister. "I know," she said. They'd both had far too little love in life. "I'm sorry. I had no right...."

After that, Kara seemed her old self again. Her spirits perked up and she began dating. In fact, she lost herself in a whirlwind of boyfriends, one after the other.

Leida, on the other hand, dated only casually. Most of the boys in town had her and Kara pegged as loose girls, so the only time Leida felt comfortable going out was when she met someone from one of the other small towns nearby, someone who hadn't heard about "those Wilson girls."

Then Kara came home one night declaring she was in love. She'd met someone even better than Tony. They began to date steadily. However, Kara was very careful never to let him pick her up at home. After her disastrous breakup with Tony, she was careful to hide where she lived and who she really was. Her latest beau was a fellow who'd just come home from his first year of college and he lived in the next town.

Everything seemed to be working out fine for Kara—until she discovered herself pregnant. That was when her life began to crumble—and Leida's right along with it.

A knock on the door broke into Leida's thoughts. She slipped the photograph of Karen into the envelope and put it in her sewing box on the end table. When she opened the door, she gasped.

"Grant!" she exclaimed. "How did you find me? What are you doing here?"

"May I come in?" he asked.

She hesitated. Her gaze trailed over him and her heart filled her throat. He was so handsome it hurt to look at him. He was dressed in a casual, white knit shirt open at the throat, white sailing trousers and white canvas shoes—appropriate waterfront attire.

She wanted to run. But there was no escape. He was standing right in front of her. She could hardly believe it, she'd been so careful about her identity. It must have been those articles in the newspaper after the rescue that enabled him to trace her to this community.

He stood looking at her expectantly. "May I?" he repeated.

"If you don't mind a bit of slumming," she quipped.

"I didn't come to see your living quarters, I came to thank you for the painting of the driftwood you sent. You really did that in a hurry."

"It was an easy subject," she said breezily.

"But I thought you were going to deliver it in person," Grant chided. He shook his head accusingly. "I thought we had an agreement."

She couldn't think of a clever retort to that one.

Grant looked down at her for a long moment with a questioning expression.

"Oh," she said awkwardly. "Please come in." She stood aside. The barge bobbed gently in the water as Grant stepped inside.

"Very colorful," Grant said as his eyes swept the interior of her weekend living quarters.

"Won't you have a seat?" she asked tentatively. Suddenly, she felt like Leida Wilson again.

But as Grant strode casually across the room and took a seat comfortably on the couch, she relaxed. He seemed perfectly at ease.

She sat in the chair opposite him. "Have you been on a houseboat before?" she asked.

Grant laughed. "Not many places I haven't been. Most people think that because I was born in a rich family—silver spoon in my mouth as the saying goes—that I've spent all my time in country clubs sipping champagne. The truth is, I grew up working on my dad's oil fields and on the ranch. I've slept in bunkhouses, under the stars, in rowboats and canoes. You name it. Once, I decided to find out what life was really all about and I knocked around the world, working on tramp steamers."

"And did you find out what life was all about?"

He grew serious as his gaze rested on her eyes. "Sometimes I think I did," he said slowly, "and sometimes I think I'm still looking...."

She became flustered, pulling her gaze from his. She glanced around, and then suddenly wondered with a feeling of panic if she had left any sketches of him lying around. Her eyes flitted to the coffee table in front of the couch where Grant was sitting.

Leida swallowed hard as she stared with fascinated horror at Grant's trousers brushing against the coffee table. On the table, turned upside down, was a sketch pad. It contained two drawings she'd been working on—Alex Carter political caricatures of Grant Hunter!

Chapter Seven

W hat?'' she asked, suddenly realizing he had spoken.

He smiled wryly. "I don't seem to be making much of an impression. You're off in another world."

"Sorry. I just had something on my mind."

"I'll try again. I tracked you down because I want you to have dinner with me tonight. I'd like to take you to a restaurant in town as a way of saying thanks for the painting of the driftwood."

"Well..." How could she think straight when Grant was inches away from the incriminating evidence of her secret—that she was his archenemy in the press, Alex Carter!

"I insist," Grant said firmly, standing up. As he did so, he took a step toward her. His leg brushed the coffee table, knocking the sketch pad sideways off the table.

It appeared to Leida as if the pad dropped in slow motion to the floor. The loose pages with the caricatures of Grant fluttered around his feet.

"Let me get that!" The words spilled out as Leida made a lunge for the sheets.

But she wasn't fast enough. "Here, I've got it," Grant said casually. He gathered up the papers, which her petrified gaze saw were still facedown. He stood up. "This looks like art paper."

"It is." Her voice sounded hollow.

Grant started to turn the paper over.

"No," she blurted out.

"Something you're working on?" he asked.

She gulped and nodded mutely.

"May I look at it?" he asked, smiling.

"Please, no, don't turn it over," she said, trying to sound casual. "I, uh, don't like for anyone to see my work before it's completely finished."

Grant gave her a quizzical look.

"You know how it is with us temperamental artists," she said weakly. "We have our little idiosyncrasies."

He shrugged and handed the sheets back to her facedown. "Of course," he smiled. "Artistic considerations must come before curiosity."

"Thank you," she said feebly.

"My pleasure." He stood looking at her intently. They were mere inches apart, the only thing separating them being a thin pad of art paper, his hand on one edge, hers grasping the other edge. Leida was suddenly disturbingly aware of the sound of her own breath, of the smell of Grant's after-shave, of the closeness of his hands... of the power of her reaction to him. Her pulse picked up tempo.

She wanted to tear her gaze away from his, to break the electric spark that crackled like sudden lightning between them. But she wanted more not to. She felt alive and vibrant, important and vital. It was an exhilarating sensation, one she was reluctant to let slip away.

They stared at each other for a long, throbbing moment, and again Leida was certain Grant was experiencing the same emotional contact. But as before, it passed so quickly she couldn't be certain the exchange ever really took place. Was it just wishful thinking on her part that this vitally attractive man felt something special for her?

Grant cleared his throat and looked at her steadily. "Now, how about that dinner?"

"I'm not dressed for dinner out," Leida said, feeling awkward. She indicated her simple blue knit top and white pedal pushers.

"It wouldn't take long to change, would it? I don't mind waiting."

"Are you sure?"

"Absolutely," he said, his tone firm. "I'm not leaving unless you come with me."

Leida slid the sketch pad behind her and backed away from him. "Just let me brush my hair and slip into something more presentable. I'll be right with you," she said tensely.

Anything to get Grant out of her houseboat and away from those drawings!

Gingerly, she backed through the kitchen. When she reached the bedroom door, she twirled suddenly and darted past it, quickly closing it behind her. Then she heaved a sigh of relief.

She changed into a simple, cool white polyester-and-cotton-blend dress with spaghetti straps that left her sun-kissed shoulders bare. Before leaving the room, she ran a brush through her thick, dark hair.

Grant drove them to one of the more picturesque dining spots in town, a huge, three-tier riverboat moored to a dock in the yacht basin. It had been piloted from the Mississippi River a year ago. With its tall, ornate smokestacks and rear paddle wheel, it was a proud reminder of a bygone era when life was slower and more elegant.

Grant took her arm as they ascended the gangplank leading from the pier to the boat. Inside, a hostess, dressed in a red and black old-time saloon-girl costume complete with lace garter, showed them to a table.

When they were seated, a waiter brought them a complimentary glass of wine and took their order. Leida decided on a gourmet seafood platter that included wild rice, shrimp, fish and crab topped by a cream sauce. Grant chose stuffed, broiled redfish.

"At this rate I'm going to have to take up jogging to burn off the extra calories," Leida said lightly as she handed the menu to the waiter.

"I don't think you have anything to worry about," Grant said. His admiring glance sent a tingle racing through her.

"Don't be too sure," she quipped. "Since I've met you, I find myself tempted by too many delicious meals."

"I noticed your houseboat has a kitchen—"

"Yes, but I stay too busy to do much cooking, and I don't see any point in stocking up on a lot of food that will spoil in the houseboat refrigerator while I'm gone the rest of the week."

"Oh? Where do you spend your weekdays?"

Questions again.

She hedged. "In the city."

He was silent for a moment. He looked thoughtful, as if considering something. "That's where you earn your living?"

"Yes."

"I see." It was all he said, not pressing her any further. He didn't even ask which city. She could see that he had decided to be tactful, careful not to antagonize her by intruding too obviously on her privacy. But she reminded herself to be constantly on guard. A few more slips like that and she'd give herself away. She recalled his warning that he was going to find out all about her. She thought with a shudder what that would mean! It would certainly bring their friendship to a crashing end. For reasons that she didn't feel comfortable analyzing, she found that prospect very depressing.

"Grant," she said, looking across the table at him with admiration shining in her eyes. Underneath the glow lurked a shadow of regret. She wanted to say she wished they'd met at another time, in another place. It was obvious he felt something for her. Whether it was a genuine feeling of attraction to her or just a sense of curiosity because of her secrecy, she didn't know. But right now that didn't matter.

He looked at her expectantly.

"I hope that whatever you may find out about me won't change what you feel for me."

He gave her one of his quizzical, searching looks. "What are you talking about?"

She searched for the right words. "You've been more than kind to me," she said. "You rescued me, took care of me, replaced my sail—"

"Which you insisted on paying for—"

"—thought about me when you came across that beautiful piece of driftwood and saved it for me, took me for a boat ride—"

Grant held up his hands. "That's enough."

"No, Grant. I want to say what's on my mind. It's important to me."

"Why?" he asked.

"Just because it is. Grant, I want you to know that no matter what happens, I appreciate everything you've done for me. I had no idea who you were on that stormy night. Even if I had known, that wouldn't have changed things—" She rattled on, realizing she wasn't making much sense. But she had to tell him in her own way that she hadn't deliberately deceived him.

Grant frowned. "You sound serious. Is anything wrong?"

"No." Did he detect the brittle tone of her voice? "I just wanted you to know that I truly like you..."

Grant's eyes brightened.

"As a friend," she added quickly, aware that she was getting into deep water.

Grant reached across the table and took Leida's hands in his. His touch was at once gentle and firm. She felt a little dizzy. "I like you, too, Leida," he said.

"As a friend," she added for him.

He remained silent at that, his eyes strangely thoughtful and troubled.

She looked at her hands in his. They felt so comfortable in the warm curve of his hands. Regretfully, she withdrew them and placed them in her lap.

Just then the waiter brought their salads and broke the mood of tension between them.

"That looks delicious," Leida said with a feeble smile. She felt a wave of sadness, realizing that this would probably be the last time she would be with him. Surely, under the circumstances, he wouldn't try to see her again. He was engaged to be married. They shouldn't be having dinner like this tonight, she thought self-consciously. It could easily start a scandal. A man in the public eye as Grant Hunter was couldn't be that careless.

"You're off in that other world again," Grant said softly.

"Oh, I'm sorry. Just wrestling with a private problem. It's not important; I'll think about it later."

Yes, she'd think about it later. Right now she just wanted to enjoy Grant's presence. She felt warm and tingly around him, both comfortable and on edge.

Leida bit into her salad. Her eyes darted past Grant, and she froze. Her heart stopped. For a chilling second, she thought she'd suffocate. There, just past Grant, stood a woman who looked just like the midwife who'd delivered her twin sister's child!

Leida's hands shook. Was it the same woman? Or was it someone who only looked like her?

Grant was chatting about something, but Leida had sliced him out of her thoughts. She felt sick. Would the woman recognize her and speak to her, perhaps ask about Karen? Would she realize she was Leida and not Kara? Or would she, like so many people in her hometown, continue to get the identity of the twins confused?

As the woman brushed by Leida on the way to a booth, Leida saw with relief that she was a stranger. But it easily could have been the same woman. Leida sighed as she realized her new identity was as fragile as a chance meeting in a restaurant. Was there no escaping the past? Would it continue to stain her life even though she was totally innocent of that old scandal back home?

Now it all came back to her again, those dark days she wanted to escape. When Kara had become pregnant, the family had hidden the truth as long as possible. But somehow people always found out about a family's secrets. Word got around town. The awful part was that much of the gossip centered around which twin was the unwed mother. People couldn't tell the sisters apart, so half the town believed the pregnant twin was Leida.

Leida was too close to Kara not to feel a sense of oneness with her sister, even at a time such as that. But she never expected to bear her sister's shame. However, the town wags made sure they both felt the sting of humiliation. "Those Wilson girls" were behaving as predicted, according to the gossips.

Kara was crushed when the baby's father refused to marry her. He disclaimed any responsibility for her condition, saying the father could have been any of a dozen guys. She held out a feeble hope that perhaps when the baby was born, if it looked like him, he might change his mind.

However, baby Karen looked exactly like Kara and Leida, with large blue eyes and curly dark hair. The midwife who delivered her wasn't even sure which twin was her patient. Everyone was so used to the girls switching places that no one could be sure which twin was pregnant.

Aunt Maizy immediately stepped in and took charge of the baby. She taught Kara how to care for the child. Karen brought joy into their lives. But the girls paid dearly for her presence. Only the roughest boys in town would have anything to do with them. Leida retreated into a shell. She spent her spare time on her artwork.

Kara, on the other hand, felt a desperate need to be accepted, to be loved. Soon after Karen's birth, she began dating again. Aunt Maizy warned her time after time that she was headed for heartbreak. But Kara refused to listen. She felt a driving need to prove to the town and to herself that boys still found her desirable.

However, her search for respectability proved futile. The boys who dated her had one thing in mind. Kara came home more than once in a rage over the way her date had treated her. Leida couldn't bear to think of the last time it had happened....

"Leida, are you all right?" Grant asked.

"What?" Leida replied, snapping back to reality with a jolt.

"Is something wrong?"

She swallowed hard. "No, why?" she asked shakily.

"You don't look well."

"I'm all right."

"No, I mean it, Leida. You look a little pale. Do you feel sick?" He reached for her hand and she let him take it. She needed the comfort.

She felt wretched. She didn't want to relive that part of her life anymore. It was behind her. Why couldn't she let it die? "No, I, uh, have a touch of a headache. It'll pass. Maybe if I drink a cup of hot tea I'll feel better."

"Certainly," Grant said sympathetically. He patted her hand, placed it gently on the table and motioned to the waiter. In a couple of minutes, a cup of steaming hot tea was placed before her. She drank it gratefully, the warmth radiating through her body, relaxing her. She felt color return to her cheeks.

Grant looked at Leida over their after-dinner coffee. She had recovered from her temporary queasy spell and looked herself again, full of life and cheerful. He found it almost impossible to pull his gaze away from the radiant, vibrant woman seated across the table from him.

He was wrestling with his own inner turmoil tonight. He was being forced to face the fact that he was getting in over his head with Leida Adams. What was he going to do about it?

He had Alice to think about. They had always known they'd marry some day. His career was in full swing. His life, his career were all laid out before him. His marriage to Alice Townsend fell neatly into the proper place. And now Leida Adams, this beautiful young artist with a strange, secret life of her own, had come into his existence with a force that was sweeping him into deep, dangerous depths.

A dozen times in the past two weeks, he had made the firm decision that it would be foolhardy to see her any more. But she had come to him in his dreams at night and in waking moments of the day, haunting him, giving him no peace, until this evening he had rashly driven to the waterfront settlement, asked questions until he found her and invited her to have dinner with him tonight.

Was he not quite ready to settle down yet, after all? Or had he found someone who'd made him doubt the depth of his feelings for Alice? It made absolutely no sense to get emotionally entangled with Leida. What did he know about her except that she was a struggling artist? He had a promising political career ahead of him. This was no time to be toying with a strange woman, no matter how fascinating he found her.

And even while he reasoned all this out, deciding that he must put an end to this impossible situation, he still couldn't take his eyes off her. . . .

"Leida," Grant said quietly. "It's been a real pleasure knowing you. If circumstances were different. . ." His voice faltered.

Her hands grew clammy. She looked away. "Yes, I know."

"Leida—"

"You don't have to say anything, Grant," she said, nervously twisting her napkin in her lap. "I've enjoyed the evening very much. We can let it go at that."

"I want you to know that you hold a special place in my. . . thoughts."

Had he wanted to say in his heart? Leida swallowed a lump that suddenly hurt her throat. "I'm glad you told me," she said.

"I wanted to tell you how I felt before I take you home." He drew a deep breath and said, "I can't see you again, Leida."

Leida blinked quickly, aghast at a sudden rush of tears that threatened to scald her eyes and spill over. "Yes, I know." Her response was almost a whisper.

"But I'll never forget you."

"Nor will I forget you, Grant." It was the most honest she'd been with him or with herself. What was the use in denying it? She was as intrigued with him as she sensed he was with her. He'd been on her mind constantly from the first moment she'd opened her eyes in the infirmary on the oil rig. He'd destroyed her ability to do her job. She'd tried to get away from him partly because of her embarrassment over her secret life as Alex Carter, but if she were honest with herself, there was a deeper, more compelling reason. She was falling for Grant Hunter, a man who belonged to another woman. It was a wrenching sensation—to realize how much she cared for Grant and to lose him in the same instant.

For a moment neither said a word. What was there left to say? Neither of them had asked to be thrown into this situation. But once fate had brought them together, there was no stopping the flood of emotions that swept them both into dangerous depths of mutual attraction.

Now they had reached a critical point. There were no more excuses to see each other. They both knew it. It was either say goodbye or risk a deeper involvement.

"Leida," Grant said, his voice husky.

"We'd better go," she said shakily, looking away from him.

He paused. "Yes," he said simply.

They left the restaurant and Grant drove her home slowly. The ride passed quietly until finally Grant spoke.

"Let me know when you get that art show," he said. "I'd like to come."

"You'll be too busy," she said matter-of-factly.

Grant didn't reply. What was there to say? It had been an empty offer. By the time she put together an art show, their lives would be worlds apart. She might be pursuing her art career in a distant city. He'd be married. Leida would just be a memory. It was a thought that wrenched cruelly.

"By the way," he said. "Remember those trees you admired on the way into town from my place?"

"Yes?"

"I took a photograph of them for you. I had it enlarged." He reached under the seat, withdrew a manila envelope and handed it to her.

"Why, Grant, how thoughtful." She was deeply touched. She opened the envelope and withdrew an eight-by-ten photograph. Grant turned on the car's overhead light so she could look at it. "I'll frame it and hang it where I can see it every day."

"At least we have something to remember each other by," he said. "I have the painting of the driftwood."

"Yes." She wanted to say so much more, but words seemed useless now.

When they arrived at Leida's dock, Grant turned off the car engine and sat in thoughtful repose for a moment. Leida knew he had to leave, but he wanted to stretch out their last minutes as long as possible. She looked over at him in the darkened interior of the car, her eyes scanning his features, trying to memorize the face she knew all too well. His image imprinted in her memory would be all she'd have of Grant Hunter after this night.

Grant turned in the seat and stared at her. "Leida." Then he looked away.

She took a deep breath. "Grant, I've really enjoyed knowing you. I wish you the best in your career and marriage."

"Thanks," he said, his voice low. "I know you mean that."

Without another word, Grant got out of his side of the car. He came around and opened her door. She gathered up her purse and the envelope that held the photograph. She felt a sudden pang of regret and sadness. Even if it hadn't been for Grant's fiancée, she was the wrong person for him to care about. With her past tarnished by Kara and her reputation as one of "those Wilson girls," she would never be fit for a young politician in the public limelight. One could never truly shake the dust of scandal free from one's footsteps. It was fitting that Grant and she didn't give in to the magnetic pull between them.

As she stepped out, Grant took her arm to help her. She looked at his fingers holding her wrist. He had strong, masculine hands. She would never forget how his touch could suffuse her body with a glowing warmth.

Grant walked with her to the houseboat. She opened the door and once they were inside, she turned to look up at him. His gaze swept over her face, lingering on her lips. He touched her chin gently with the tip of one finger and tilted her face up toward him.

"Goodbye," he said so softly she barely heard him. Then he bent down, his lips drawing closer and closer to hers.

Leida's breathing became ragged. She closed her eyes against a fresh rush of burning tears.

Gently, Grant's lips touched hers. It was a tender kiss, the pressure of his lips as light as a butterfly. She felt suspended in time. She wanted this instant to last forever.

But the kiss ended, and Leida could see a terrible struggle in his eyes.

He couldn't find the willpower to take his arms from around her. There was an agonizing moment that lasted an eternity. Then with a sudden, choked cry, he drew her closer and his lips found hers again. But this time he couldn't restrain his hunger. His mouth pressed desperately against hers and her arms slipped around his neck.

He whispered her name against her lips. "Leida...Leida—"

Her breath was coming in ragged gasps.

"Leida, I didn't plan for this to happen," he said brokenly. "I was just going to say goodbye and leave—"

"I know," she whispered.

They gazed into each other's eyes seeing the raw hunger unmasked there. With a cry, his lips sought hers again. Her lips parted, surrendering to his deeper kiss.

His hands were moving over her, seeking the supple outlines of her back, her sides, her hips, igniting fires wherever he touched her. Then his kisses sent a trail of fire from her mouth to the hollow of her throat. She gasped when his trembling fingers slipped the straps of her dress down over her arms and he kissed first one bare shoulder, then the other. Her dress fell to her waist. She closed her eyes, her head dropping backward. Strength was melting from her body.

His kisses found her breasts. Her nipples throbbed and burned with the touch of his lips. She sobbed as desire became a blazing fire out of control, raging through her body. There was no strength left in her legs as she melted into his strong, passionate embrace.

Then, with a broken cry, he wrenched himself away from her. There was the sound of the motor, the furious grinding of the rear wheels on the shell road, and then only sight of the taillights vanishing in the darkness.

Leida sank in a sobbing heap on the deck of her houseboat.

Chapter Eight

It was a week later.

Grant Hunter radioed the airport control tower from his private Lear jet and brought his plane in for a smooth landing at Dallas International Airport.

Beside him sat his fiancée, Alice Townsend. He had flown from Austin to her family's ranch in West Texas. Alice had suggested they make the short air trip to Dallas to dine at their special restaurant, which served exquisite French food prepared by a master chef from Europe.

Grant had often thought that by any sensible reckoning, Alice Townsend was the woman designed for him. A graduate of Vassar, she was as intelligent as she was beautiful. She had traveled extensively, had all the proper social graces, wore smart, stylish clothes and seemed to delight in the social whirl that accompanied his entry into politics. She was an expert at entertaining his colleagues and could join intelligently into political conversations. She never pressured him to spend large blocks of time with her when he was embroiled in his political entanglements. In fact, the only time she'd ever really demanded anything that made him uncomfortable was when she'd attempted to pin him down to a wedding date.

The airport limousine whisked them to their destination, a restaurant in the penthouse of one of the city's tallest buildings. The view of the city lights from the twentieth story windows was breathtaking.

When Grant and Alice entered, the efficient maître d' showed them to their table immediately and snapped his fingers impatiently for a waiter. The service was impeccable, the setting plush. Chairs were upholstered in soft leather. The tables were covered with imported Irish linen. The china, crystal and silver services were the finest Neiman Marcus could supply. A string group played a muted musical background. Complimentary iced champagne was brought to the table, in the center of which was a spray of fresh red roses.

As they sipped before-dinner cocktails, Alice asked, "How is the campaign going?"

A brief frown shadowed Grant's brow. He thought about a phone call he'd gotten this morning from his campaign manager, Clayton Brooks. "Not too good. Clayton's worried."

A look of concern crossed Alice's lovely features. She reached for Grant's hand, gave it a sympathetic squeeze. "Poor darling. I could tell you have something on your mind. You haven't spoken ten words since you picked me up." She laughed. "And that's not like you. You may be a tall Texan, but you're definitely not the silent type."

He smiled wryly. "Sorry. I guess I'm not very good company tonight."

It was true he was wrestling with a heavy mental weight, but for the moment, the problem was not politics.

His gaze took in his attractive, stylish companion. But he had trouble keeping her in focus. Persistently intruding was the ghostly image of blue eyes with swirling, secret depths, a smooth complexion slightly tanned by the sun and windswept, dark hair. Leida's image haunted him. He couldn't escape thoughts of her—day or night. That was the real reason for his preoccupation tonight.

Alice said, "I noticed that the hostility from the newspapers had eased up a bit after all that publicity about your rescuing the woman, but now they're back after you with a vengeance. That series of political cartoons they're running is downright vicious."

"Yeah," Grant said smoothly. "That Alex Carter trash. That guy really has it in for me. It's like a personal vendetta with him. I hope I can meet him someday. I'd be sorely tempted to break his face."

The meal came. Grant poked at his food, barely touching it. His dark, silent mood persisted throughout the meal.

The dishes were whisked away. After-dinner brandy was served. Again he felt Alice's cool, soft fingers give his hand a squeeze.

"Grant, I'm worried about you. I've never seen a political campaign get you down like this."

He drew a deep breath. His troubled gaze met her green eyes. "Alice, it's not the campaign."

A slight frown stenciled her smooth brow. "Then, what in heaven's name is it, darling? You're getting me upset. It looks as if you've lost weight. There are lines under your eyes as if you haven't been sleeping well. You're not ill, are you?"

He smiled wryly. "Not physically." He sighed, "Alice, for the past couple of weeks, I've been at war with myself. You're right about my not sleeping."

He thought back to the last time he'd seen Leida. He could still feel their kiss burning his lips, that explosive moment when her body was close to his, trembling with a promise of passion that inflamed his blood and gave him no rest. He could keep nothing on his mind except the exquisite secrets hidden beneath the cool summer dress she had worn that night. In his ears was her soft voice, growing husky with passion as he had held her closer and their kiss had deepened.

He took a sip of his brandy, feeling its warmth touch his lips and trace a burning path down his throat. He directed his troubled gaze again to Alice's eyes. "We have to talk, Alice. That's the real reason I called you for this date tonight...."

Leida strolled along the water's edge, her thoughts tumbling in her mind. She tried to draw a measure of solace from the burnished rays of the setting sun. The huge orb spread its fading light across the gently stirring water of the gulf, casting a treasure of silver diamonds sparkling on its surface.

Leida stopped and spent a long time staring into the distance, her gaze scanning the horizon where blue-green water gently kissed dusky blue sky. A scattering of sailboats headed for shore, their sails almost limp from the lack of a breeze.

She looked down at her bare feet where the warm saltwater lapped lightly at her toes. She saw a sand dollar and bent over to pick it up and examine its surface. It was perfect. There were no nicks or breaks in its delicate structure. It was round, with the little holes in its shell in just the right places. She thought vaguely of the legend of the sand dollar, the story about the tiny shapes inside the shell that resembled doves. Too often people were so intrigued with the interior of the sand dollar that they broke it open to shake out those dove-shaped pieces, in the process destroying the integrity of the shell as a whole.

She felt like a sand dollar that had been shattered. Since Grant had come into her life, nothing had been the same. She should be on her houseboat this minute, working on another painting for her collection, but she knew the effort would be worthless. She hadn't been able to touch a paintbrush for the past week. Her concentration was in tatters. Every time she sat down to paint, she found herself staring off in space, her mind flooded with memories of Grant.

When she thought about the passionate kiss they had shared that last night they'd been together, a hot flush spread over her entire body. A storm of emotions churned through her. At times she hated Grant for arousing that kind of passion, only to walk out on her. But then she had to admit that she admired him for the strength he'd shown. She sensed that he had wanted her desperately that night, and it had been obvious that she couldn't resist him. But if he had carried her into her houseboat and made love to her, he would have betrayed Alice, the woman he was engaged to. Not many men had that kind of integrity, but Grant did. For that she had to respect him and love him all the more. It made the hurt of losing him even greater.

Yes, she had to admire Grant for breaking off contact with her. Keeping her feelings about him under wraps had been one of the hardest tasks she'd had to tackle in a long time. But she could no longer avoid the staggering truth that she had fallen in love with Grant Hunter, head over heels, hopelessly, impossibly in love with him. How she longed to tell him! How desperately she'd wanted to hear him say he loved her! But that was impossible. He had made it perfectly clear that he was never going to see her again. The physical attraction Grant felt for her might be powerful, but it didn't mean he actually loved her.

A tear trickled down her cheek. Perhaps things had worked out for the best. Aunt Maizy always said that no matter how bad life became, one could learn valuable lessons from the hard times. In fact, she had insisted that there was always an element of good in every life event.

Perhaps the good in Leida's short but disastrous relationship with Grant was that he'd avoided becoming involved with the likes of her. Grant had a brilliant career ahead of him. He was made for politics. He could take the blows that went along with the job.

What kind of political future would Grant have if he associated with Leida? She knew how the media worked. People in the public eye had practically no privacy. Had Grant been seen with her, the muckrakers of the press would have tried to dig up all the dirt they could find on Leida Adams.

How would it have looked for Grant to be squiring around a woman with a sordid past, even if that past was the result of her being confused with her twin sister? Who would believe Leida was an innocent victim of a small town's malicious gossip?

She hadn't been able to convince the hometown folks that she wasn't Karen's mother or that she hadn't run wild, frantically looking for love after the baby was born. Everyone thought both of "those Wilson girls" were scum. No one could be sure which was which nor did they care.

So, any romantic inclinations between her and Grant had been hopeless from the start.

Leida stood on the beach, the tears trickling down her cheeks, her face drawn and sad. She'd coped with knottier problems and had survived. She'd survived this, too. She just wished it didn't hurt so much.

She realized that it had grown dark while she wandered along the beach. She glanced down at the sand dollar in her hand, its beige surface glowing in the silver light of the moon. When she looked up, she saw a figure far down the beach, half-obscured by the misty haze that perpetually hovered over the water's edge. When the figure drew nearer, she saw it was a man. He was striding in her direction. Was he, too, seeking solace from loneliness?

Leida watched the shadowy form grow larger. There was a familiarity about him. Was it his long, deliberate stride, his broad shoulders? She shook her head to clear away the image.

But when she looked again, he was still coming, and as he neared, she realized she knew him.

She gasped, her voice catching in her throat. In shock, she dropped the sand dollar. It hit the hard, packed sand with a whisper, shattering its outer shell.

Moonbeams danced around Grant's dark brown hair. He slowed as he neared her, his steps tentative.

"Leida?" he said softly.

She was too shocked to speak.

"Oh, Leida," Grant said huskily. He stood right in front of her, towering over her, looking down into her wide eyes. An eternity passed in a second as he gazed intently at her. He took her hand in his and kissed the tips of her fingers.

"What are you doing here?" she asked. "Is something wrong?"

"Not anymore," he said.

She thought her heart would burst. She didn't care why he had come. He was here, and that was all that mattered. She felt so complete with him, so fulfilled, and yet there was a deep longing for more, more of him, more of them together, something deeper, wider, more intense, more permanent.

"I want to talk to you," Grant went on, a strange excitement in his voice.

He took her arm and they walked slowly along the water's edge. "I guess things happen in life that we don't plan," he murmured, as if half to himself. He paused. "Leida, do you understand what I'm trying to say?"

"Not exactly," she whispered, still half-dazed.

He stopped to face her, slipping his arms around her, drawing her gently closer. Her heart thundered in her ears.

His voice husky with emotion, he said, "I care a great deal for you, Leida. I don't know how strong your feelings for me are, but—" He sighed. "Last week, I tried to say goodbye. I thought it would be best for both of us. I haven't had a moment's peace since. I just can't bear the thought of not seeing you again. Leida, I've fallen in love with you. Do you understand? I love you, my darling."

"Y-you what?" she gasped.

"I love you. This isn't a sudden thing. It's been growing in me since the moment we met. I tried to tell myself it was merely an infatuation, a physical attraction that would pass. But the more I was around you, the more dear you became to me. This past week has been hell. When I told you last week that I couldn't see you, that I had to say goodbye, I thought I could put you out of my life, but I simply can't. I can't live without you Leida. I can't say goodbye. That's the decision I came to this week."

"Oh, Grant, do you mean it?" she choked. Could she dare believe what she'd heard?

"Of course I mean it." He pulled her into his arms and crushed his mouth down on hers, draining away all doubt. His lips were almost feverish with passion.

Leida squeezed him tightly, her arms hugging him possessively, as if he might escape. She returned his kiss with all the fire she had in her, attempting to express her deep love for him.

They held the kiss a long time, their lips melding, his tongue gently probing her mouth. Steamy sensations pulsated throughout her body. She melted even closer to him, her body conforming to his contours as if they'd been made expressly for each other.

Finally, he pulled away. Her lips felt bruised, her breath heavy, her lids half closed. Dreamily, she heard him say her name, "Leida. Do you feel the same about me?"

"Yes, my darling. Yes!" It was a half whisper. "I love you, too. I think I have since the first time I saw you."

They looked deeply into each other's eyes, stripping away the layers they'd worn to protect themselves from their true feelings. They saw past the facade for the first time, each feeling lost in the depths of the other's visual embrace.

"Leida," Grant said softly. "Leida. I want you. Do you want me, too?"

"Of course, but...."

For a second, the past with its ugly memories intruded on the beautiful moment ... the hurt when she knew boys dated her only because of the reputation she and Kara had in the town ... the times Kara had sobbed herself to sleep because she had been treated like a cheap tramp. She shivered, suddenly growing cold, and she drew back from Grant.

"Leida, I'm not asking you for an affair. I said I love you. I want to marry you."

"Marry me?" she repeated in a dazed voice.

"Yes, Leida. I want you to be my wife. I want to share the rest of my life with you."

"Oh, Grant," Leida said tearfully, melting into his arms. He kissed her again, a long, deep, slow, passionate kiss.

When it was over, Leida's senses were reeling. However, she still had a shred of sanity left. "What about Alice Townsend? You and she are engaged."

"Not anymore. I had to tell her how I feel about you, Leida. I had to break the engagement. It wasn't an easy thing to do. I didn't want to hurt her, but it would have been more cruel to marry her knowing I didn't love her, that I love you. Leida, I've been restless and dissatisfied with my life lately. I think part of it was because deep down I didn't really love Alice, but I wouldn't admit it. Since I met you, I've felt the entire range of emotions in a way I haven't felt in years, all the way from the heights of joy to the depths of despair. It's been painful at times, but worth it because I'm tasting life to the fullest again. Alice was shocked, of course, when I broke the news to her, but once she's had time to think it over, she's going to realize I was right."

Grant drew her closer, looking directly into her eyes. "Will you marry me, Leida?"

Leida laughed and almost cried at the same time. "Oh, yes, Grant, yes. Of course I'll marry you."

He scooped her up in his arms and kissed her again, as if he couldn't get enough of the sweet taste of her lips.

Leida returned his kiss, pouring out all her pent-up emotions. Somewhere in a distant part of her mind there was a dark cloud that had something to do with her past as "one of those Wilson girls," and mixed in with it were the ugly Alex Carter cartoons she had drawn . . . but all that was far off and almost obscured by the radiant happiness that engulfed her. If it was something she had to worry about, she'd think about it another time.

"Grant, have you lost your mind?" demanded Clayton Brooks.

During the lull after Grant's announcement, Clayton's ruddy face turned a deep red and he gnawed the stub of his cigar. He seemed momentarily at a loss for words but then he popped up from behind his desk at the campaign headquarters and flung Grant a shocked look.

"No, I haven't lost my mind." To himself, Grant thought, *I've lost my heart*.

"Well, if you ask me, you sure as thunder have. You know you may be tossing the election right into your opponent's lap, don't you?"

"I'm sure we can handle this, if we just keep our heads," cut in Carl Hunter, Grant's father. He was standing behind Grant near the door, thoughtfully watching the exchange between his son and Clayton Brooks. At age sixty, Carl was a handsome man, with a full head of wavy white hair that contrasted with rugged, deeply tanned features. He was slightly shorter than Grant and heavier, but his face had been chiseled from the same basic mold as Grant's. He was a Texas version of Cary Grant, dignified, suave and cool.

"There's nothing to handle," Grant said to his father. Then he directed his attention to his campaign manager. "Clayton, don't be so dramatic." Grant brushed aside the man's concern. Brooks was one heck of a campaign manager, perhaps the best in any state in the union, but it took a cool politician to deal with his emotional outbursts. The man expected perfection. To Clayton, winning the race took precedence over everything else in life. He expected his clients to adopt the same dog-eat-dog attitude. Clayton milked every political strategy known to push his man to the top.

Clayton barged over to Grant and halted in front of him. He wasn't the least bit intimidated by Grant's superior height. At five foot six, Clayton barely reached Grant's shoulders. There were rumors that the man wore elevator shoes, but no one knew for sure.

If Clayton was sensitive about his size, he never let on. He was as feisty as a bulldog and twice as threatening. His impatience and intense drive had earned him two mild heart attacks. Instead of slowing his pace as his doctor had ordered, Clayton, at age fifty-five, seemed determined to live twice as fast as ever to cram all he could into the rest of his life.

His glittering blue eyes burned with the fire of a tough political fighter. He was ruthless, cynical and demanding. He had no patience with those who crossed him.

"Dramatic? You think I'm being dramatic?" Clayton asked hotly. "Just look around you, Grant. See those campaign posters over there with your photograph?" He pointed through the glass wall of his office to a long table behind which sat a spate of volunteers who answered the phone, handed out campaign literature and helped round up crowds for political rallies. Plastered all along the wall behind the tables were huge posters with Grant's smiling face, proclaiming him a man for all the people.

Grant nodded.

"Maybe it's going to take something or someone dramatic to make you realize that this is not a Sunday school picnic. This is the real world, Grant, a world where the slightest misstep could cost you the election. This race is not a shoo-in. Your opponent has attacked you with a hatchet. The latest polls show you trailing. If the election were to be held this minute, you'd lose. You know how rough Texas politics can be. One slip, and your opponent will string you up by your thumbs."

"Clayton, sit down," Grant ordered firmly.

The man sniffed, obviously agitated, but took a seat. Grant found a chair for himself. The senior Hunter remained standing.

"Clayton, I've merely changed my mind about marrying Alice Townsend. Is that political suicide?"

"Then it's true," his father observed. "I could hardly believe it when Alice told me." He looked deeply thoughtful.

Clayton picked up the conversation. "Grant, what's come over you? Alice is the perfect choice for your wife. You've known her all your life. You come from the same kind of background. She's a superb hostess. She plays well in the press. She's every politician's dream wife. She'll be an asset to you the rest of your life."

Grant frowned. "Clayton, I don't want to marry an asset."

"Why not? It makes perfect sense. Alice is the woman for you." He paused, scowling. "She said you'd found somebody else. Is that true?"

Grant nodded.

"What do you know about this woman, Grant?" Carl asked, his voice calm and his words measured, a marked contrast to Clayton Brook's agitated staccato style.

"Enough."

Clayton popped out of his chair. "What do you mean enough? Give me some facts. Who is she, where's she from?"

Suddenly Grant felt exasperated. "Clayton, she's not an animal with registration papers."

Clayton began to pace.

Carl spoke up. "Son, I think it would be wise for us to know something about this woman."

"She might be out to ruin you," Clayton pointed out. "She could be a spy from the other camp."

Grant laughed. "Clayton, she's not that kind of person. She's the woman I rescued from the gulf. Our meeting was entirely accidental. She's not a plant."

Clayton narrowed his eyes and gave Grant a hard look. "Never assume, Grant Hunter. I learned that long ago in this business. This may be only a state race, but your opponent has his eye on the big time, just as you do. The winner of this campaign could very easily be headed for the governor's mansion and then the national scene. Never underestimate the lengths to which the opposition will go to make you look bad."

Grant sighed. "I wish Alice had kept her mouth shut."

Clayton turned red again. "You mean you weren't going to tell me?" he blustered.

"In time."

"Grant, you *have* lost your mind. As your campaign manager, you know darn well I have to know every move you make. You're leaving yourself wide open to a personal scandal. Don't you see how this is going to look to the voters? The dashing Senator Grant Hunter jilts his fiancée for a last-minute replacement. This kind of thing before the election could spell disaster. The opposition will love that. The gossips will have a field day."

Clayton paused, gnawed on his cigar a moment and jabbed a finger toward several of the latest political cartoons pinned to the wall. "You'll sure give that cartoonist Alex Carter a lot of fresh material!" Then his eyes narrowed thoughtfully. He sank back into his chair, lacing his fingers over his vest. "Okay, so let's accept the fact that you're infatuated with this woman. I can understand that. I've gone a little goofy a few times in my day. That's why I don't have any money in the bank now. Take a little man-to-man advice from a guy who cares about your future. Have a little fling with her, but be discreet about it. You'll have her out of your system in a few weeks and get your sanity back."

Up to that point, Grant had listened to his campaign manager's raving with a degree of amused tolerance, but now he came close to losing his temper. "I don't seem to be getting through to you, Clayton. I love Leida. I don't want any kind of cheap affair with her. I want her to be my wife."

Clayton Brooks rolled his eyes heavenward and threw up his hands in a gesture of helpless exasperation.

"I'm sure Grant is not going to do anything rash," Carl said in a soothing tone, stepping over to his son. "He's too smart for that. His political career means too much to him. What we need to do is discuss this situation in a rational manner and decide how best to proceed. Too much is at stake to jump into anything."

"Dad, I'm sorry. But there's nothing to discuss. I've already made up my mind about Leida. I'm going to marry her soon. It's that simple. Now, if you two will excuse me, I have things to do."

"Well, son," the elder Hunter said, "you're an adult so I can't tell you what to do. I can only advise you not to rush into something hasty. You could put off your marriage until after the election, couldn't you? That wouldn't be asking too much, I don't think. If your young woman loves you, she'll understand."

Grant frowned thoughtfully. "I don't know, Dad. I'll think about it. We haven't set a definite date yet."

His father smiled. He clapped a hand fondly on his son's shoulder. "Give it serious consideration, Grant. Your mother and I were engaged for a year before we were married. In this case it wouldn't be nearly that long. Just until after the election, that's all."

Grant said, "Dad, all I can promise is that I'll think it over." He nodded at Clayton and Carl and left the room.

Clayton slumped in his chair, holding his head in his hands, a look of defeat etched into his features. "We're sunk," he moaned. "This is going to cost him the election."

Carl strode to the window, looked out pensively for a moment. He said softly, "When Grant was born, I asked only one thing of fate—that I live to see my son in the governor's mansion." Then he turned to Clayton. "We can't allow Grant to make a mistake he'll regret for the rest of his life, Clayton. Let's find out all we can about this woman. You know how to handle such an investigation."

Clayton looked up, his defeated expression fading, replaced by a sparkle in his small eyes. He looked thoughtful and nodded, his lips curling in a cold smile. "Yes," he said simply, rubbing his palms together.

Chapter Nine

The aroma of prime rib roasting to a succulent medium rare curled around the kitchen and wafted to Leida's nostrils as she checked the evening's supper. Since returning to the houseboat the day before, she'd stocked up on groceries and had gotten out her best cooking utensils.

She wanted the evening to be special and perfect. She'd taken out the linen tablecloth Aunt Maizy had insisted she take with her when she'd left home.

"It belonged to my mother," Aunt Maizy had said. "Using that cloth on special occasions always made her feel genteel. There'll come a time when you'll want to impress somebody. Take the tablecloth, honey. It's got a special magic. You'll see."

In addition to the ecru tablecloth, Leida had splurged on an arrangement of fresh flowers to accent the table. She didn't have silver cutlery or china place settings, but Grant never seemed to mind. It was amazing how well he fit into any situation, how he was comfortable and at ease wherever they went, whatever they did.

She glanced out the houseboat window and her pulse rate suddenly accelerated as she saw Grant's sports car pull up outside. She smiled, her heart swelling with love. She pulled off her yellow apron and smoothed out her apricot-colored blouse and dark brown skirt. The colors beautifully complemented her flawless complexion.

The past two weeks since Grant proposed had been like a romantic fantasy. More than once, Leida had pinched herself to check if she was dreaming. She felt like Cinderella going to the ball. Whenever he could steal a little time from his campaign schedule and legislative duties, Grant would swoop down in his private jet and spirit Leida off to an intimate, romantic date. Once they had flown to New Orleans to share a meal on the patio of a famous French Quarter restaurant. Another time they had flown to San Francisco's theater district to enjoy a play.

They had not yet set a date for the wedding. Leida was perfectly willing to wait until after the election in November. She was enjoying the romantic courtship and the adventure of getting to know Grant Hunter. Every time they were together, she found out something new about him, and she became even more convinced that the newspaper she worked for was totally wrong. He was not the selfish, materialistic political animal her editors had painted. Grant, Leida had concluded, was a brilliant legislator, an honest, sincere man, deeply concerned about not only his district but also the welfare of all the people in the state, no matter how rich or poor.

That had brought up the painful dilemma of how to break the news to Grant that she had drawn the vicious Alex Carter political cartoons. Sometimes the confession was almost on her lips, but she recoiled in fright. Grant's discovering the truth about her when he was so emotionally involved with his campaign could destroy their relationship. He would be furious and unwilling to listen to any explanations.

No, she had decided, she must wait. She would never draw another Grant Hunter political cartoon and she'd try to bury the ugly truth about her political cartoons. Some time in the future, when the dust and fury of the political campaign had settled, perhaps after they'd been married for a while, she would tell Grant the truth.

At times she felt a stab from her conscience about keeping the secret from Grant, but she defended her decision, telling herself that she'd had such little happiness in her life. The love she and Grant had found was so precious to her—more important to her than life itself—and she would do almost anything to protect it.

She remembered how furious her editor, Sam, had been when she broke the news to him that she was through drawing political cartoons attacking Grant Hunter.

He had stormed around his office. "That's gratitude for you! I make you a rising star in the political cartooning arena, and you stab me in the back."

"I'm sorry, Sam," Leida had replied. "I just can't do it anymore. I feel like a terrible hypocrite. I simply don't believe the things your editorial writers say about Grant any longer."

"Oh, now it's 'Grant.' Just as I suspected. You've got a crush on the guy, right?"

A lot more than that, she thought. I love him. But she didn't put her thoughts into words. Grant was not quite ready to announce their engagement because of the possible political repercussions. If she blurted out to Sam that she was in love with Grant Hunter and they were engaged to be married, he'd break his office door down getting to the newsroom to release the story in the next edition. No, for the moment Leida preferred to keep her private life to herself.

Sam went on, "I hate to see you get in too deep with that guy, Leida. You won't be the first to fall for the Grant Hunter charm and wind up getting your heart broken."

Leida flushed angrily. "That's just some more of your political gossip-mongering, Sam. Grant Hunter is not that kind of man. I simply don't believe the rumors about his romantic conquests. Grant is a decent, honorable man."

Sam threw his hands up in exasperation. "Believe what you want to!" He snorted. "Right now you've got stars in your eyes over him. One cold morning you're going to wake up and find out what we've been saying about him is true. Then you're going to wish you'd made him even uglier in those caricatures."

"I doubt that," she said coldly. "And you're not changing my mind, Sam. I am through drawing political cartoons about Grant Hunter."

"Do you realize what you're throwing away? You're getting statewide recognition with those cartoons. Pretty soon you'd be able to syndicate nationally. You're tossing away a brilliant future like you're quitting a copy boy's job."

"There's no use trying to persuade me, Sam. My mind is made up. I'll do cartoons about national issues, but no more state politics. It would probably be better all around if you'd find someone else to take my place to do all the Alex Carter drawings."

"That's going to be difficult," the editor muttered darkly. "You have a style that won't be easy to duplicate. The public will be able to tell that somebody else is drawing the Alex Carter cartoons. You realize you're leaving me in the lurch right when the campaign is starting to heat up?"

"Yes, I know." She sighed. "I've agonized over that, but I just don't have a choice. I'm sorry."

"You're not half as sorry as I am!"

"If you want to fire me, I'll certainly understand."

"That's not going to get me any more of your cartoons," he grumbled, "although at the moment it would give me a great deal of pleasure. No, we'll find something for you to do in the art department. Maybe you'll come to your senses!"

As she was leaving his office, Sam got in a parting shot. "You can forget about that raise I'd promised you!"

On the weekend, Leida stopped at a fast-food restaurant for a hamburger and then drove to the coast, growing more excited by the minute as she thought about her plans for Saturday night. It was the first time she'd invited Grant to a home-cooked meal on her houseboat.

The drive to her houseboat seemed interminable. She was eager to leave the city behind and to prepare for Grant's arrival. She daydreamed about the romantic evening ahead of her, about nestling in Grant's strong, protective arms, listening intently to his description of his week, offering him her undivided attention.

She hurried to the door and opened it just as Grant was about to knock.

"Hi, darling," Grant said, scooping Leida up in his arms. His mouth came crushing down on hers. She felt light-headed, intoxicated and was filled with an inner warmth, an inner glow.

The kiss had taken her breath away. When she was able to talk, she said, "Come, darling." They walked arm in arm over to the couch.

Grant settled on the couch with a contented grin, drawing Leida closer. She snuggled into his arms. "Tell me about your week," she said.

"Oh, there've been an assortment of political rallies and speeches. I addressed a group of university graduates, who asked some very intelligent questions.

I think I persuaded a few I'm not the knave in black armor some of them thought I was. Then I spoke to a gathering of retired people who are naturally concerned about issues affecting them. After that, I gave a pep talk to a bunch of kids from all over the state attending a government workshop in Austin. I was impressed with how articulate those young people were. I signed a few autographs for them.''

"A boost to the old ego, huh?"

"I'll say. Usually some jerk like that cartoonist, Alex Carter, is trying to get my head on a platter.''

Leida blushed. She felt like sinking through the floor. Thank goodness Grant wasn't looking at her. Guilt must be written all over her face!

"A woman from *Texas Monthly* called for an interview,'' Grant went on, "which I scheduled for next week, and I spent some time on the oil rig.''

"Sounds like a busy week," Leida said.

"Yes. I'm looking forward to relaxing with you tonight and to dinner. I'm tired of the rubber-chicken circuit.''

Leida giggled. "And I thought I was so clever to have cooked you chicken for dinner,'' she said with mock ruefulness.

Grant cocked his head to one side. "The aroma coming from your kitchen doesn't smell like that of roast chicken.''

She threw up her hands in surrender. "Just teasing," she said lightly.

"Woman, there's a cruel streak in you I've just seen for the first time,'' Grant quipped. "I think I better kiss it away before it gets any worse.''

He pulled her to him and kissed her. The touch of his warm lips sent hot blood coursing through her veins. She gasped as his fingers slipped open the buttons of her blouse and sought the delicate curve of her breast.

After a long moment, she pulled back breathlessly. "Keep that up and I'll forget how to finish cooking the meal," she said thickly, buttoning her blouse.

He gazed at her, his eyes smoky with desire. "That might not be so bad...."

With an effort, she drew her reeling senses back into order. "Grant, don't tempt me. Dinner's almost ready." Then she added, gazing directly at him, her eyes filled with promise, "But afterward, we have the whole evening—"

He made a grab for her, but she darted just out of reach.

"That's not fair, after what you just said!"

"What I just said was wait until after the meal. Meanwhile, how about a tall glass of something full of ice to cool you down a bit?"

"It'll take more than that—"

She tried to run to the kitchen but he took two long strides and captured her, his strong arms drawing her closer, setting her heart pounding again.

"Unhand me, you cad," she said breathlessly, "or I'll report you."

"Nobody reports the captain," Grant replied.

"This is my boat," Leida reminded him playfully, "so I happen to be the captain of this tub."

Grant chuckled and Leida smiled back, filled with joy. She'd never dreamed loving someone could make her feel this complete. When Grant was away, she experienced a loss so great she felt like only half a person. Grant had become the spark that gave her life its full meaning. She couldn't imagine her life without him.

She checked on supper, saw that the prime rib was ready and put the last items on the table. She was glad she had an assortment of vegetables for Grant this evening. After the description of his week on the rubber-chicken circuit, she knew he'd appreciate the change. He'd already told her how much he liked fresh vegetables, and she'd cooked squash, green beans and okra. She wanted to please him, to make him as happy as he made her.

Over dinner Grant told her how the campaign was progressing. "It's going to be a close one, I'm afraid. You see, I have to run on my record. There have been issues I agreed with in principle, but I've had to vote against some very popular bills because there were provisions tacked on that made them outrageous. Votes like that give my opponent a handy target when he attacks me. Since he's a newcomer, he's running on an untried platform. He has no voting record to attack. It's easier for him to make me look undesirable to the voters."

Leida was concerned about the lines of worry and fatigue around Grant's eyes. She smiled, wanting to make an effort to get his mind off his worries. "Why don't we forget politics tonight?"

"Good idea." Grant leaned back in his chair, patted his stomach and grinned. "Tell me how you learned to cook so well."

Leida felt her cheeks color. "Actually, I'm a miserable cook," she admitted. "My neighbor, Dora Marshall, came over this afternoon and helped me prepare dinner. Without her help, this meal might have been a disaster."

Grant tossed her a suspicious glance, as if he didn't quite believe her.

"It's the truth, Grant."

"Holding out on me, hmm?" he asked. "Is there anything else you haven't told me?"

Leida looked away a moment. She bit her bottom lip. She felt guilty but she couldn't tell him the truth just yet. Hastily, she added, "Don't worry, I'm going to learn how to cook. When we're married, I want to be able to prepare special meals for the two of us."

"There are a lot of special things that you can do for me without learning to cook." With that, he pulled her to him and gave her a long, slow kiss that turned her muscles to water.

"I see what you mean," she said breathlessly.

"Maybe we can learn to survive on love alone," Grant said huskily.

"I don't mind if I do," Leida replied, her eyes half-closed.

Just then Leida heard a knock at her houseboat door. She started. She couldn't imagine who it could be. Dora certainly wouldn't intrude on her evening.

Grant looked up, then in the direction of the door.

"Just ignore it," Leida said, slipping onto his lap. She put her arm around his neck.

"Gladly," Grant said, pulling her to him. Before his lips touched hers, the knock came again, this time louder and more insistent.

"I think your caller is determined," Grant muttered.

"Okay," Leida conceded. "I'll answer it. But I'm going to send whoever it is packing in short order."

Grant nodded approvingly.

Leida opened the door to a small, blue-eyed man in a neat gray suit.

"Good evening," the man said with a short nod. "I'm Clayton Brooks, Grant Hunter's campaign manager."

Leida was momentarily too surprised to answer.

"You must be Leida Adams," he went on, giving her a steady look.

"Yes," she replied. His hawklike eyes made her uncomfortable. She wondered what could be so important that he'd come to her houseboat to locate Grant. How did he know where she lived? Had Grant told him?

"May I come in?" he asked. "I know Grant is here."

"Why yes." Leida nodded. Just then Grant strode up behind her.

"Clayton. What are you doing here?" Grant asked with a touch of annoyance in his voice. "And how the devil did you find me?"

"I checked with your housekeeper, Mrs. Garcia. She said you were on your way over here for the evening. I need to talk to you, Grant."

"Can't it wait until tomorrow?" Grant asked, obviously irritated.

Brooks shook his head. His voice was grave. "No, Grant. This is important. It can't wait."

"All right," Grant sighed. He apologized to Leida, "I won't be long," he said. He took a step toward the door.

Clayton blocked his path. "We need to talk inside. This concerns Miss Adams, too."

Leida felt a sudden chill of apprehension. The look in the campaign manager's cold blue eyes sent a shiver through her.

Grant frowned. "What do you mean by that?"

"Take my word for it," Clayton replied. "I'll explain."

Grant glanced at Leida. She swallowed hard. She'd taken an instant dislike to Clayton Brooks. But she could hardly refuse to let him in. She nodded and motioned the man inside.

Clayton stepped in, closing the door behind him. He glanced around the houseboat, then at Leida. He studied her for a moment, then turned his attention to Grant.

"I think we'd all better sit down," Brooks suggested.

Leida said, "If you two want to talk in private, I can do some things in the kitchen—"

"No." The campaign manager gave her a peculiar look that sent fresh chills shooting all over her. "I think you should be here, Miss Adams," he added, staring intently at her.

She swallowed.

"For heaven's sake, Clayton," Grant said, obviously annoyed, "let's get to the bottom of this. You're interrupting what had been a very enjoyable evening."

They walked to the living area and found a place to sit. Leida joined Grant on the couch, feeling a strong need for his protectiveness. She didn't like Clayton Brooks and suspected the feeling was mutual. The campaign manager sat in the chair opposite them.

Grant said impatiently, "Well?"

Clayton shifted his gaze from Grant to Leida and back again. "I've been doing some checking, Grant," Clayton said slowly, his words carefully chosen, his speech deliberate and grave. "I've uncovered something disturbing, something you should know about immediately."

"Go on," Grant urged.

"I know this is going to come as a shock, but I have no choice. I have to tell you what I've found out. It can affect your future in public life, Grant. You know I've been worried about some directions your private life has been taking lately—"

A flush of anger spread over Grant's face. "Clayton, dammit, your job is to run my political campaign, not butt into my private life—"

Clayton Brooks gave Grant a cold look. "A public official has no private life, Grant. You've been in politics long enough to know that."

There was a moment of strained silence as the two men's eyes clashed.

Then Brooks said, "The past two weeks have been very enlightening. I've made some interesting and rather surprising discoveries."

"Get to the point," Grant snapped.

"All right." Brooks nodded. "You are familiar, of course, with the political cartoonist, Alex Carter."

"Well, certainly. Why?"

Leida felt a sick knot in the pit of her stomach.

Brooks asked, "Have you ever met the cartoonist, Alex Carter?"

"No, of course not. The paper won't reveal his identity. You know that."

Brooks nodded slowly. He pursed his lips. "Would you like to meet Alex Carter?"

The blood was pounding in Leida's ears like a bass drum. Her throat felt constricted. She found breathing difficult. "Grant—"

Her voice was faint. Grant seemed not to hear her. He was staring at his campaign manager with a puzzled expression. "You're not making a whole lot of sense, Clayton, you know that? I don't understand what you're trying to do. This was supposed to be a private evening, so if you don't mind—"

"You haven't answered my question. Would you like to meet Alex Carter?"

"What would be the point in that? The guy obviously hates my guts. I'm not too fond of him. Why should I want to meet him? What would that prove?"

Brooks shook his head, looking grave. "In that case it might prove very interesting. It took some doing, but I've discovered the identity of Alex Carter."

Leida choked. Her hands turned clammy. She felt dizzy.

Before she could protest, Clayton spoke again. "I have contacts at the Austin newspaper. Alex Carter's true identity has been a closely guarded secret, but my contact got to the truth."

The campaign manager turned to Leida. "Would you care to tell Grant the truth, Miss Adams? Or shall I?"

Grant's expression was one of increasing bafflement. "What has Leida got to do with all of this?"

"Why don't you ask her?"

Grant's puzzled gaze turned to Leida.

Leida felt paralyzed. With a great effort, she forced her lips to move. "Grant, what he's trying to tell you is that I'm the person who has been drawing those awful political cartoons. I am Alex Carter."

Her voice sounded distant and faint to her, as if she were hearing another person speaking.

For a long moment, the room seemed frozen in time. There was no sound, no movement. Through a haze of tears, Leida saw a number of expressions cross Grant's face—everything from puzzlement to stunned disbelief. He shook his head slowly, like a half-dazed fighter who had just received a stunning blow.

"I—I don't understand."

Leida sighed. "Grant, it's very simple. I can't support myself yet with just painting; I got a job on the Austin paper some time ago, in their art department. Their political cartoonist quit and I got the job of drawing the political cartoons for their editorial page."

Grant said nothing for a moment. Then he turned to Clayton. In a choked voice, he said, "Clayton, I need to talk to Leida alone."

Brooks nodded. "Of course. I understand." He popped out of his chair and strode quickly to the door.

After he left, there was a deathly silence. In it, Leida could hear her heart pounding. She felt drained of all emotion.

Grant stood looking at her, fury raging in his eyes.

"Grant, I can explain," she said.

"There doesn't seem to be a whole lot to explain," he said coldly.

"I was going to tell you," she said.

"When?" he demanded.

"After the election."

"You deceived me, Leida. You've been pretending to be in love with me and the whole time you've been laughing behind my back." Grant began pacing the room, his fury mounting. "Clayton and my father tried to warn me that you could be a political spy working for my opponent. I wouldn't believe them. What a fool I was!"

"Grant, that's not true!" Leida exclaimed, hurt and angry. "I haven't drawn any more of those caricatures since we met."

"I don't believe you. There was one in the paper this morning."

"I drew that several weeks ago. They have an inventory, a backlog of those drawings."

"How can I believe anything you say, now? If you wanted to be honest with me, why didn't you tell me long ago?"

"Yes, I should have," she admitted. "I was afraid. I wasn't sure how you'd take the news. You made so many scathing remarks about Alex Carter."

"And you let me make a fool of myself."

"No, I didn't see it that way."

Grant stared at Leida with an expression she'd never seen before. "It's not only the cartoons, though it's beyond me how you could draw something that vicious about someone you claim to love. The part that has me angry is the way you've been lying to me ever since you met me. Leida, why weren't you honest with me?"

"Grant, you're being unreasonable," she retorted, her cheeks flushed. "What I did wasn't so awful. I already had the job when you rescued me. I was just trying to make a living."

"That's not the point," Grant flung back at her. "You deceived me, Leida. You know how hard I've been working on this campaign. You know the slightest misstep could mean the difference between winning and losing the election." His voice began to rise. "I trusted you, Leida."

Suddenly, Leida started to get angry. "Trusted me!" she shot back. "You told me you were going to find out all about me, remember? If you trusted me so much, why did you set your watchdog, Clayton Brooks, on my trail?"

"I didn't tell Clayton to investigate you," Grant retorted hotly. "That was his own idea. But if you'd been honest with me, there wouldn't have been anything to investigate!"

"If I'd been honest with you, you'd have acted just like this!"

"No, Leida. I could have forgiven you your job, if you'd been willing to quit once we became involved. What I can't forgive is your deception."

"I didn't purposely deceive you, Grant."

"What do you call it," he demanded irately, "when you refuse to tell me the truth about yourself? I asked you, Leida. I asked you directly, more than once, to tell me about yourself. You gave me that cagey little story about being a struggling artist whose big goal in life was to have an art show. Hell, Leida, I could have arranged for you to have twenty art shows!"

"I don't want a show I have to buy my way into!" she snapped. "I want my work to stand on its own."

"You certainly got your wish with those Alex Carter cartoons," Grant fumed. "They've been in the newspaper every week since we met. You can't tell me you weren't still turning them in."

"My editor has been using caricatures I drew before I met you!" she shot back. "You don't believe a word I say, do you?"

"Why should I?" Grant retorted. "You lied to me."

"I didn't actually lie," Leida said heatedly. "I just didn't tell you everything, which I realize is not being honest, and I apologize. But I'm telling you the truth now—I stopped drawing those cartoons after I fell in love with you."

"I don't see why I should believe you," he said coldly.

Leida backed away from him, half-blinded with tears and anger. "Is your love so shallow that when I need your understanding you turn against me? You don't believe me when I try to explain; you've taken your trust from me without even listening to my side."

He shook his head slowly, his expression cold and distant. "Leida, I don't know what to believe about you anymore."

"Then I guess there's nothing more we can say to each other," she said, her voice breaking. "Obviously, you don't trust me anymore. Without trust, how can a relationship go on?"

She turned her back to him and blinked back hot tears of regret.

She waited a moment, hoping Grant would come to his senses and try to understand. Instead, she heard his footsteps heading for the door.

She turned just in time to see him grab the doorknob. "I'm washing my hands of you, Leida. I never want to see you again!" He bolted through the doorway without saying another word and slammed the door behind him.

She ran to the window and watched as Grant jumped in his car, backed away from his parking place and roared off in a cloud of sand.

Leida moved away from the window and went into the living room area. She sank onto the couch and buried her face in her hands. Low, racking sobs tore from her throat.

Chapter Ten

Leida turned onto the main street and drove slowly past the wooden frame buildings. In front of the barber shop a couple of elderly men sat in the shade, talking and nodding slowly. A deserted auto-parts store was boarded up, just as it had been when she'd left town. From the looks of it, nothing had changed.

She had been on the road all day, ever since she left her houseboat early this morning. Now, late in the afternoon, she was driving slowly through the streets of her hometown. She was tired and gritty from the long drive, but she was barely aware of her physical weariness. The anguish of her emotional state pushed physical awareness aside.

She had spent a sleepless night, torn apart over her quarrel with Grant. Early this morning, as the sun sent

its first streaks of fire across the rippling water surrounding her houseboat, she had come to a decision.
Staying there after what had happened was impossible. It was too painful. Everywhere she looked, she
saw Grant. Everything she saw reminded her of the
ecstasy she had known in his arms. Never again would
she be able to sail in her little boat without the
wrenching pain of memories. She had lost all desire to
paint the waterfront scenes she had once loved.

She felt an overpowering need to flee, to put this
bittersweet episode of her life far behind and make a
new start.

After the long night filled with tears, Leida had
made her decision. She could quit her job on the
newspaper and bury herself completely in her art, im-
mersing herself so totally in her painting there would
be no room left for the pain of Grant's memory. She
had been putting aside a small nest egg of savings. By
counting her pennies, she could survive on it for some
time. Where she would go, she wasn't yet sure. She
wanted to see Kara's little girl, Karen, and Aunt
Maizy, so she would make her hometown her first
stop. Then she would hit the road until she found a
place where she'd want to stay and paint.

It hadn't taken long to throw a few belongings in her
car. She had looked back once at her houseboat,
seeing it through scalding tears as memories swamped
her, then on to Austin where she settled her business
matters. She didn't feel guilty about leaving her job at
the newspaper on such short notice. Now that she was
no longer drawing the political cartoons, they had no
great need for her services. The art department could

easily find a replacement. As for the few belongings in her apartment, she turned them over to a friend to dispose of.

Then, with her bridges burned behind her, she headed for the piney woods section of East Texas and her hometown.

As she drove, the heartbreak of loving Grant Hunter washed over her with renewed, intense pain. Last night when the quarrel ended in bitter words and Grant stormed off her houseboat, she had been as much angry as hurt. But now her anger was drowned in the aftermath of grief—the terrible finality of knowing she would never see Grant again, that she had lost forever the one man she would ever love so completely, so desperately.

She rubbed the back of her hand across her eyes, dashing tears aside to clear her vision so she could see the road.

Bitterly, she thought that whoever said it was better to have loved and lost rather than never to have loved at all didn't know what the heck he was talking about! She wished she had never met Grant Hunter. Then she would have been spared this wrenching pain.

Now she could fully understand how devastated Kara had been over her tragic love affair. There was nothing more painful than to love another person with all your heart and soul, to let that love fill all your dreams and hopes, and then have it all turn to ashes.

Now, on the main street of her hometown, Leida pulled into the service station next to the grocery store to fill her tank with gasoline. Lanky Peters sauntered out to her car, pulled a dingy red rag from his pocket and wiped his damp brow. He was a tall, lean man in his late sixties. When he was younger, he'd spent many a night at Jim Wilson's bar, drinking and carousing.

"Evenin', miss. Fill her up?"

"Yes, Lanky, thanks," Leida said, getting out of her car.

Lanky cocked his head to one side. "Why, if it ain't one of those Wilson girls," he said, grinning toothlessly.

She felt a sudden wave of anger. She raised her chin and looked straight into his eyes. "No, Lanky. I'm not 'one of those Wilson girls.' I'm Leida Wilson."

"Well, now, I reckon I never could tell you two apart," he said slowly.

"Kara died, remember?" Leida said tersely, staring right at Lanky, demanding her rights as an individual.

"Well, sure," he said. "I'm sorry."

"I'm sorry, 'Leida,'" she corrected him.

He looked at her with a strange glint in his eyes, as if he were seeing her for the first time. There was a note of concession in his voice. "I'm sorry, Leida," he said. He hesitated, as if wondering if he'd satisfied her. Then he opened the flap over her gas tank and began to fill it with gasoline.

He probably still didn't know which twin she was, Leida thought. But it really didn't matter. She was surprised at how little she cared what he thought.

"I ain't seen you in a long time. I heard you left town. You back to stay?"

"No. Just for a visit."

Lanky smiled and glanced at the pump. Then he looked back at Leida, screwing his lined face up in a grimace. "What do you hear from that brother of yours, Jeff?"

A momentary feeling of shame threatened to spill over Leida. But she fought it. "I haven't heard from him since he left," she said frankly. She wasn't going to be ashamed. Her wayward brother was a fact of life. It was that simple. If anyone asked her about him, she'd openly acknowledge his behavior without so much as a shred of embarrassment.

"Never did think much of that boy," Lanky rambled on. "He was a bad one from the start."

Leida didn't reply, but she didn't hang her head as she once had. She looked Lanky squarely in the eye and smelled the clean, clear air. Never had the aroma of her hometown smelled so sweet. She remembered the environment here as oppressive, dreary. Actually, it was a quaint little town, surrounded by beautiful, huge pines stretching majestically toward the sky. The air was pure and invigorating. She could actually have enjoyed the atmosphere if she hadn't been so heartbroken over Grant.

Leida paid Lanky for her gasoline and drove on, this time heading for the little cemetery on the edge of town. She felt new waves of sadness as she drove through the iron gates, but there was none of the old feeling of shame. She stopped near a row of grass-covered graves and got out of her car.

She took a deep breath and walked slowly toward the plot with the simple marker "Kara Wilson." Her throat tightened. A tear trickled down her cheek.

"Kara," she said softly. "I've forgiven you. It wasn't until I fell in love that I understood how powerful love can be. I didn't understand when we were in high school. You never knew it, but for a while I hated you for dying and leaving me to carry the burden of your shame. It was childish of me. I've grown up now. I'll always miss you, and I'll always love you."

She stared into the distance, not seeing the stately pines surrounding the cemetery grounds. Instead, she recalled her last memory of Kara.

Leida realized now that the father of Kara's child, a young man named George Barton, had been the great love of Kara's life. Kara was not a bad girl or a loose girl the way the town wanted to believe. She had just loved too intensely, too generously, not stopping to count the cost.

For a while after the birth of her child, Kara had been pretty wild, dating a string of boys, staying out too late, drinking too much. But then she settled down to going with one boy. He was the only one who seemed to genuinely care about Kara. Leida remembered his name was Jim. She had hoped that there was going to be a happy ending to her sister's troubled life. But poor Kara... the dark star that guided her destiny would not relent.

One night Kara had taken their father's pickup to drive to another town to meet Jim when he got off work. They had gone to a dance at a country hall. During the evening, there had been some trouble. From what Leida could piece together, the father of Kara's daughter, George Barton, showed up at the dance. Kara had never gotten over him. When he asked her for a dance, she went into his arms without hesitation. Jim got angry and left. Then George turned all his attention to another girl, ignoring Kara. Alone and rejected again, Kara had stormed out of the hall, jumped into the pickup and raced away.

The highway patrol found the pickup smashed into a bridge near a dangerous curve. Kara had been killed instantly. Had she driven too fast and failed to see the sharp curve...or had she reached a dead end in her life where she no longer cared and saw the bridge as a way of ending her troubles? Leida would never know.

After Kara's death, Leida began to think about leaving her home. As had so often happened before, many people in the town had her mixed up with Kara and believed it was Leida who'd had the child out of wedlock. That mistaken notion was reinforced when the gossips saw Leida caring for Kara's child. Later, when Leida moved away, there was cruel talk that she had callously abandoned her illegitimate child.

It was Aunt Maizy who had advised her to use her talent for a ticket out of this town. Leida would forever be grateful for that bit of advice.

Those hours she'd spent drawing and painting as a means to escape her unhappiness had paid off. She earned a scholarship to college that was the start of a new life.

Now, as Leida returned, she realized she had changed. She was more mature, sophisticated, confident. And she no longer felt ashamed of who she was. Here she might be Leida Wilson again, but it was a Leida Wilson who held her head high and felt proud. It was a good feeling. She valued herself for what she was and for what she'd made of her life. What other people thought of her didn't matter one bit. It was what she thought of herself that counted.

Leida left the cemetery and headed in the direction of her old home. On the way, she passed the pizza joint where the school kids had hung out. She remembered the "in" crowd, and how she and Kara had always been outsiders.

She passed the variety store where she'd tried to get a summer job while in high school. Old Man Vickers had shaken his head, avoiding her eyes. "Sorry, Leida," he'd said. "My wife just wouldn't put up with it. I don't have anything personal against you, you understand. But the missus, she wouldn't hear of hiring a Wilson."

But that was all history. She had to live in the present. She drove on, crossing the railroad tracks, following a bumpy, narrow road that led down to the river. A flood of memories and sensations swept over her. She took a deep breath to steady herself. Her old home seemed totally foreign to her. In fact, she realized she'd never felt she belonged here. However, her parents were still running the bar in front of the living quarters where she'd grown up, and she was going to see them while she was here. She didn't expect much of a reception.

Later, Leida drove to Aunt Maizy's house. Her aunt no longer went out to work. She'd retired to collect social security and take in sewing. With that and the extra money Leida sent her, Aunt Maizy had been able to rent a small frame house in a quiet neighborhood.

Both Leida and Aunt Maizy agreed it was a more suitable home for Karen to grow up in.

Aunt Maizy spread her arms wide and gave Leida a bear hug. "Oh, honey, you're a sight for these tired eyes," she said cheerfully.

Leida held on to Aunt Maizy for a long time before she let her go.

"Let me look at you," Aunt Maizy said, her voice wavering. "What a wonderful surprise!"

They were standing in the small living room of Aunt Maizy's house. The wooden floors were scarred, the area rug worn, but the place was spotless.

"Where's Karen?" Leida asked anxiously.

"She's visiting a friend." Aunt Maizy beamed.

"She has friends?"

"Since I moved away from the river, Karen has been able to make a few friends. It's done her a world of good. It hasn't been easy. You know how folks in these parts are. They don't want their kids playing with a child who doesn't have a pa. I've tried to protect Karen from ugly comments. Gossip is mean."

"Then she'll be all right with you a while longer?" Leida asked.

"Yes," Aunt Maizy said, stepping back and motioning Leida to the sofa. Her blue eyes were paler now but still spoke volumes about her inner iron strength. "She's a fine child, Leida. But she's going to need a permanent ma and pa one of these days." She sat down in the rocking chair. Leida took the couch.

"I didn't know you were coming. I would have had her here." Aunt Maizy smiled. Then she frowned. "You been by to see your folks yet?"

Leida nodded mutely.

Aunt Maizy waited patiently.

Leida shrugged. "It was the usual," she said dryly. "You'd think I'd just been gone to the corner store for a carton of milk. Mama seemed kind of glad to see me, but Pa was too wrapped up in one of his customers to notice me much."

Aunt Maizy rocked slowly. "That brother of mine," she muttered. "That don't reflect none on you, honey."

Leida smiled. "I know, Aunt Maizy. I used to think it did. I felt I couldn't be very lovable if my parents didn't love me."

"They love you in their peculiar way. They just don't know how to go about showin' it."

"I finally realized that, too," Leida said. "But you've always been more like a parent to me, Aunt Maizy."

"I always considered you my own, Leida—you and Kara." A tear filled the older woman's blue eyes. Then she looked directly at Leida. "Honey, I got a feelin' something's wrong," she said gently. "You want to tell me about it?"

Leida looked down at her lap, struggling to hold back the tears. Then she sighed. "Oh, Aunt Maizy, I feel so miserable."

The large woman got up from her rocking chair and joined Leida on the couch, wrapping an arm around her. She let Leida cry as she patted her comfortingly.

Through her tears, Leida spilled out the whole story of her disastrous love for Grant Hunter.

Aunt Maizy listened patiently. She sighed. "Yeah, honey, I know all about man trouble. I've had my share of it. What you need is some time. Broken hearts don't mend overnight. What you need to do now is to stay so busy you don't have time to think about how miserable you are."

"Yes," Leida agreed. "I quit my job in Austin. I think I'm going somewhere to paint. It's what I really want to do. If I can work full-time on it, I think I'll be good enough to interest an art gallery in showing my work."

"Can you afford to do that?"

"I have a little money saved; enough to last for a while."

"Do you have someplace in mind?"

"No. I thought I'd decide that after I saw you and Karen. Do you have any suggestions?"

Aunt Maizy looked thoughtful. "Ever think about Mexico?"

Leida shook her head slowly. "No, I hadn't."

"I've got a friend who lives in Reynosa, a town just across the border. I could put you in touch with her. She could help you find a little place where you could live and paint."

"Mexico," Leida said thoughtfully. "Yes, that might be just the place."

"Thanks, Carmen," Leida said, pushing past the front door, her arms laden with canvases, paint-brushes and other art supplies.

Carmen nodded and smiled, rushing behind Leida to help her with her load.

It was hot and dry in Mexico. The dust swirled from the small street outside the courtyard wall that separated the cluster of small, ground-floor apartments and tiled patios from the rest of the world.

Leida had had no trouble locating Carmen Gomez, Aunt Maizy's friend. The small, dark-haired woman had welcomed a relative of Aunt Maizy with open arms, treating Leida like a long-lost cousin. There was a vacant apartment next to Carmen's, which Leida rented immediately. Carmen helped Leida cope with the Mexican way of handling such transactions. Then Leida began moving in. Between her chores of washing clothes, running after two small dark-eyed grandsons, and sewing, Carmen helped Leida unpack her car and settle into her new abode.

The quarters were simple, which was fine with Leida. She strode across the tile floor of the beige stucco apartment. The living room walls were plaster, each a different bright color—blue, orange, yellow, red—that gave the small area a cheerful atmosphere. The furniture was a light hardwood with decorative upholstery. The arch-shaped windows were covered with black bars, a distinctive feature of Mexican buildings.

Leida carried her first load on through an arched doorway, into a large room with a double bed in one corner, a bedside table, a dresser and a window with a view of a lovely courtyard garden. She was surprised at how cool the interior of the structure felt.

Leida unpacked the rest of the car rapidly. She felt too numb inside to be affected by the last heat wave of summer that scorched the dusty streets and sent the entire nation into an afternoon siesta to escape the blistering rays of the sun. She had one driving goal—to lose herself in her art.

As soon as she had unpacked her art supplies, she slipped into a pair of sandals and a sleeveless summer dress, and pulled her hair back high on her head and fastened it with a clip to keep the thick strands off her neck.

"You sure you're going to be all right?" Carmen asked as Leida prepared to leave. The woman was standing at the front door of Leida's apartment, eyeing her grandsons as they played with a ball and stick in the courtyard. There were several small children laughing and chasing each other.

"Thanks, Carmen, I'll be fine," Leida said, smiling. "You've been a big help. I really appreciate it."

"De nada," Carmen replied, brushing aside Leida's gratitude. "But if you need me for anything, I am just next door. Call anytime."

Leida nodded. "I'll remember that. And don't worry, I'm not the bashful type. If I need help, I'll ask."

Carmen smiled and then cast a baleful eye in the direction of her grandsons. She muttered something in Spanish and hurried over to separate a tangle of small children scrambling in the dirt.

Suddenly, Leida felt desperately alone. She was in a foreign country whose language she didn't speak. She had no telephone. She couldn't read the Spanish newspaper or understand the programs on her radio or the portable TV.

She took a deep breath. Yes, life was different here in Mexico. But that was why she had come. She needed to get away, to lose herself. In Mexico, she could do just that. Already she'd seen countless scenes she was desperate to paint.

She left her apartment and walked across the courtyard, sketch pad under her arm. Out in the narrow streets of the border town Leida was sharply aware of the sights and smells of her new environment. She noticed the aroma of corn husks and onion. She heard a dog barking in the distance. On the street she saw a door-to-door vendor pulling a wooden cart. A young boy was dragging a stubborn burro behind him with a frayed rope. At the corner a battered bus pulled up to a stop, its interior bursting with humanity. An elderly woman carrying a cage of chickens slowly boarded. From the back door spilled several young men in colored cotton shirts and knee-length breeches. One clutched a shiny acoustic guitar to his chest. They hurried off down the street, talking rapidly in Spanish.

Leida frowned. In spite of all she saw around her to paint, the gnawing, empty feeling of her heartbreak over Grant kept recurring in waves. She concentrated on her sketch pad, losing herself in the scene she was drawing. She had to draw—now, this instant. She had to dull the emotional pain. This was the only way for her to do that.

She took a deep breath. It was hot. She needed to find a cool spot, perhaps under a tree somewhere.

How long Leida sketched she didn't know. She was oblivious to the curious stares of passersby. She drew

furiously until she ran out of paper. She noticed with
a start that it was growing dark. It was long past sup-
pertime, but she had no appetite. She slipped her
sketch pad into her oversize purse and hurriedly found
her way back home. She set up her easel in the living
room and began to transfer one of her scenes to the
canvas, drawing madly, splashing streaks of paint
across the surface, working late into the night until her
burning eyes could no longer see her work clearly.

The next morning she rose early and repeated her
trip into the town, her eyes feverishly scanning the area
for new scenes to draw. This time she brought an extra supply of art paper and an assortment of colored
chalk. She located the open market where merchants
sold handmade wares such as pottery, jewelry, wood
carvings, leather goods, hand-sewn clothes and Mexican artwork. She stood in the narrow aisle between
the heavily stocked booths, sketching rapidly, glancing at the lines she saw before her and transferring
them to her paper. She duplicated the colors, the
shapes, the textures of what she saw.

For the next three weeks Leida's life was a blur of
frenzied drawing and painting. She ate little, walked
a lot, observed constantly and never stopped working. Her apartment grew crowded with paintings. As
she finished each one she put it aside and began the
next. Sometimes she worked on two or three paintings simultaneously, suddenly switching from one to
the other when an idea for a new stroke or color hit
her.

Carmen brought over homemade tamales and guacamole along with *menudo* and stacks of tortillas.

Leida thanked her neighbor profusely, but only nibbled the tasty treats. She shoved most of the food in the refrigerator and scooped it up the next day to distribute to the eager little children who sold gum on the streets to help out at home. For her trouble, Leida bought Carmen several bags of groceries.

She had no time for checking her appearance in the mirror. Had she done so, she would have found that her face had grown thinner, her eyes feverish.

One evening, when she'd stopped her frenzy of activity to assess her latest work, she heard a commotion in the courtyard outside her window. Dogs began to bark. There were the high-pitched giggles and excited chatter of small children.

Leida ignored the sounds as she cast a critical eye at her painting. It was good—much better than anything she had done before. She'd captured a touching scene of an old man wearing a limp, gray sombrero hobbling down the street on a crooked cane. Next to him walked a small child, her face beaming with love, as she helped the older man on his way.

Leida had seen this very tableau only a few days before. She couldn't forget the look of simple resignation in the eyes of the old man. Yet, from those tired eyes a spark had glistened for an instant when the small child, probably a granddaughter who dearly loved her grandfather, had offered him her most prized possession, a ragged doll. It was a scene of great compassion and love.

Vaguely, Leida was aware of a knock at her door.

"Just a minute, Carmen," she called out. She wiped her hands on a rag and backed up to the door, gauging the impact of the painting from her greater distance. Yes, it was definitely the best work she'd ever done. The emotion her earlier paintings had lacked vibrated from this canvas. She could almost hear the old man and the little girl speaking to each other.

Mechanically, Leida gripped the doorknob and twisted it, her eyes still captured by the canvas. She pushed on the door and, without looking at her caller, said, "Come on in, Carmen. I want you to see this."

The voice that responded made her heart stop. Her blood suddenly turned cold, chilling her.

Leida twirled, a silent gasp on her lips. She looked directly into the face of Grant Hunter!

Chapter Eleven

Leida couldn't speak. Her senses reeled. She grew frightened, thinking her tormented emotions had caused her mind to snap and she was having a hallucination.

But the hallucination would not go away. She drew a ragged breath, blinking her eyes, willing the mirage to vanish. But there he stood, all six feet of him, broad shouldered, tanned, his intense, brown-eyed gaze fixed on her.

Then she heard his voice as if from a distance. "Leida." Worry lines etched his brow as his gaze scanned her from head to foot. "You're so thin. You look as if you've been ill—"

Leida felt the muscles in her legs dissolve. She swayed. With a soft cry, Grant reached out to catch her, but she fought off the wave of blackness and drew back.

Her mind was not playing a cruel trick—it really was Grant. A tumult of emotions stormed through her. She struggled with an impulse to laugh and cry at the same time. Her first instinct was to rush into his arms and shower him with kisses. But then the memory of their quarrel and bitter words formed in her mind.

"What are you doing here?" she asked, her voice shaky. "How did you find me?"

"May I come in?" Grant asked.

Suddenly she felt a wave of anger and a desire to slam the door in his face. Instead, she just stared numbly at him.

"Leida, I have to talk to you."

"I think we said it all," she replied soberly.

Grant took a step toward her. She recoiled from him.

"Leida, don't, please," he said gently.

She turned, unable to look at him anymore. She swallowed hard, fighting to hold back the tears. She was amazed that her bruised emotions were capable of reacting. She thought she'd died inside.

To get away from him, she withdrew to the other side of the room, stepping around canvases that were propped all over the place. She hugged the far window, gazing out at the patio, desperate for Grant to leave, yet miserable at the thought that he might.

Out of the corner of her eye, Leida saw Grant rub his hand through his hair. He seemed at a loss for words. He looked around the room for a moment.

"I see you've been painting."

How inane! Of course she'd been painting. She remained mute.

"These are very good, Leida."

He walked slowly around the room, taking his time as he viewed her work one by one. It was some time before he spoke. "In fact, they're excellent. I don't think I've ever seen a series of paintings with such depth. It's as if I'm seeing past the people on the canvas right into their souls."

Leida turned, her face registering surprise. Was her work that good? Was he being honest with her? "Do you really mean that?"

He stopped and looked across the room at her. "Yes. They're beautiful, haunting. There's such beauty and such pain. It's a powerful combination."

Leida shrugged. "I just painted what I saw—and what I felt," she said, with emphasis on the second phrase.

Grant looked at her steadily, a troubled expression on his face. There was a long, silent moment and then he said gently, "Leida, I came to ask you to forgive me."

A part of her wanted to cry out, "Yes, I forgive you, my darling." But the words wouldn't come. "Don't you think it's a little late for that?" she said coldly.

"I hope not, Leida. I realized almost at once that I'd made a terrible mistake. I'd been working hard campaigning, facing an opponent who's using every dirty trick he can to cut me apart. I've been on edge, on the defensive for months. When I found out you were Alex Carter—well, something in me snapped. I was hurt, angry. I lost my temper, said things I shouldn't have. I'm afraid I didn't handle it very well."

"Grant, you can't just walk in here, apologize and expect everything to be like it was before. That night you made it clear you didn't trust me anymore."

"I shouldn't have said that," he admitted.

"But you did."

"It was stupid of me, Leida. I let my ego and resentment push me into a dreadful mistake. The next morning I came to my senses. I rushed back to you, but you were gone. No one knew where you went. I went to the newspaper in Austin and they told me you'd quit and left town without saying where you were going. You had simply vanished off the face of the earth. I almost went out of my mind. I had to find you."

"After what you said, I find that hard to believe," Leida retorted icily.

"Leida, it's the truth." He took a step toward her, but stopped when she moved back.

"I hired the most prestigious private detective in Texas to locate you. You didn't leave much of a trail. It took him weeks to find you. He finally called me early this morning, telling me where you were. I dropped everything, got in my car and rushed right here."

Leida felt herself tremble. A bitter struggle was raging inside her. "Grant, if you said you didn't trust me then, how do I know you'll ever trust me completely? Don't you see how important that is to me?"

"Leida." His tone was imploring, insistent. "We can't let it end this way."

"Perhaps it's already ended," she whispered sadly.

"It hasn't if we don't want it to," he persisted.

Leida shut her eyes against her inner turmoil. She heard Grant's footsteps approach. "Don't!" she snapped, stepping backward. She shot him a threatening glance.

Grant halted.

"Leida, we had a special relationship. We felt something for each other that comes along maybe once in a lifetime. We can't throw that away. I've been almost insane with regret since I walked out on you. I don't blame you for hating me. But underneath the hate, there has to be still a glimmer of love!"

Leida shook her head, but she knew she was denying the truth. Of course she still loved him. But he'd rejected her. Everyone she'd ever loved, except Aunt Maizy, had rejected her. That night of the quarrel, when he'd said bluntly he thought she was lying, that he didn't trust her, it had shaken something deep within her, it had cracked the foundation of their relationship. Perhaps his words had been spoken in anger. But could she believe that? How could she be convinced that trust was again restored?

"I don't believe you when you say you don't love me anymore, Leida."

Could he so easily read her thoughts? She couldn't lie to him again, so she said nothing.

"You love me," he went on, "in spite of yourself."

He stepped toward her. This time she stood her ground, staring at him with tears swimming in her eyes.

"I don't want to be hurt like that again," she said in a hoarse whisper.

"You won't be, I promise." He drew closer.

"Loving you is too risky," she protested.

"The only risk you take is that I might spirit you away to the bedroom and never let you go."

The tears spilled over and trickled down her cheeks. "No, Grant. It just won't work."

He was in front of her now. He took her hands in his and caressed them tenderly, slowly pulling her closer to him.

"Why not, Leida?" he asked.

"Because you haven't convinced me that you really trust me now. Love just isn't enough without that—"

"How can I convince you?"

"I don't know. I guess it takes time."

He slipped an arm around her. She tingled all over. But she held her body rigid.

"Then I'll take whatever time is necessary. We can make it work, Leida," Grant whispered in her ear, "if we want to."

She wanted to, wanted to in the worst way. Why not just throw her arms around him, kiss him and say all was forgiven? Her arms ached for him. But he'd wounded her so deeply.

She could understand how he'd felt when he'd learned the truth about her. In his place, she might have reacted the same way. But to allow herself to love him again was to invite the possibility of more heartbreak. This time she had to know that whatever happened, she could always rely on him. She wasn't yet convinced.

Grant touched her chin and tilted her face toward his. Her countenance remained expressionless. Slowly his lips neared hers, closer, closer. A shudder ran through her.

"No," she choked, pulling away. She twisted from his arms and turned her back to him. "Grant, please, just go away and leave me alone. Don't stir up those feelings again. I don't want to love you anymore. I just want to forget you."

There was a moment of silence. Then Grant spoke. "Leida, if I thought you really meant that, I'd walk out that door and you'd never see me again. I want you to be happy."

She stood with her back to him, her shoulders slumped, expecting any minute to hear his footsteps retreating, deserting her. But he stayed.

"Leida, I know I said cutting things to you. I didn't mean it. It was my pride talking. It was only because I love you so deeply that I felt so angry when I thought you'd deceived me. Don't you understand?"

Slowly Leida turned to face him. She recalled how angry she'd been when Kara had died. Angry because someone she'd loved so much had hurt her so deeply. Tears stained her cheeks. She nodded silently.

"Then you forgive me?"

For a moment she didn't react. Then the tears spilled over. "Yes," she said faintly.

"Oh, darling," Grant replied huskily. He took a step toward her as if to sweep her up in his arms.

She pushed a restraining palm against his chest. "But that isn't enough."

He gave her a questioning glance. "You still love me, don't you?"

She swallowed hard and nodded. "Yes, but Grant, I can't turn my emotions on and off like a water faucet. It's been so long—weeks—that I've been trying to get over you. I have to have a little time to get used to the idea that we're now back together again. I'm not ready to fall back into your arms right now."

Grant looked thoughtful. "Of course," he said. "I'm expecting too much, too soon. I've been so frantic to find you. I hurt you terribly, Leida. You don't know how sorry I am. Let me make it up to you."

"Not now, Grant. I just want to be alone for a while. You go on back to the States. After a time, I'll come back and we can see if there's really anything left of our relationship."

Grant shook his head. "No, Leida, I'm not letting you out of my sight again. I'm not leaving here until you agree to come with me."

"That's very flattering, Grant," Leida said, her tone polite but cool.

"I'm not trying to be polite, Leida. I'm trying to show you how serious I am about my feelings for you. I'm not going to make the same mistake again."

"Grant, I can't go with you yet. It would be hypocritical of me to pretend the pain never existed. I've spent the past few weeks trying to get you out of my system, convinced it was all over between us."

"Then I'm staying here until you're ready to go back with me," Grant announced. The determination in his voice convinced her he wasn't kidding.

"Staying where?" she asked.

Grant pointed to the floor. "Right here!"

"In my apartment?"

"That's right," he affirmed.

"B-but," she spluttered.

"No buts, Leida. I'm not leaving. I don't care how long it takes, I'm not letting you out of my sight. I came to Mexico to take you back with me, and I'm not about to return home empty-handed."

"All right," she said, "you can stay. But you're sleeping on the couch."

Grant looked disappointed, but nodded.

"It's lumpy," she pointed out, "and hard."

"I'll manage," he replied resolutely.

"There's no air-conditioning."

"I can take the heat."

"Noisy children play in the courtyard on the patio early every morning."

"I love kids."

"I'm not going to wait on you," she pointed out. "You'll have to take care of your own meals, making the couch up for a bed, that sort of thing."

"I'm used to taking care of myself."

"Good. There's food in the refrigerator. Help yourself to whatever you want."

"I think I'd better take you somewhere for a decent meal," Grant said.

"What's the matter?" she challenged. "Are you too good to rustle up your own supper?"

"No," Grant commented. "But judging from the looks of you, if I depend on your refrigerator, I'm liable to starve. You've lost weight, Leida."

"I haven't felt like eating," she defended herself. "It's too hot to eat." The truth was she'd been too miserable over Grant to eat.

"Well, we're going to take care of that right now," he exclaimed. "Come on, I have my car outside. Let's find a good restaurant and start the process of getting you filled out again."

"Wait just a minute, Grant Hunter," Leida spouted off. "You can't come in here and take over, telling me what to do."

"Somebody needs to take care of you," he retorted. "You need a keeper." His tone turned more serious. "Whether you like it or not, you're eating a decent dinner tonight, even if I have to feed you a forkful at a time!"

With that he took her by the arm and led her toward the bedroom. "Now change into something appropriate and be back here in ten minutes, or I'll renege on my agreement to sleep on the couch."

"Why, you . . ." Leida spluttered, only half-angry.

She hurried into her bedroom and shut the door, then dug in the closet and found two sheets. She gathered them up along with a pillowcase that she stuffed with a blanket, took them into the living room and shoved them in Grant's arms.

"Here," she said. "You might as well make up your bed while I'm dressing. This is the best I could do for a pillow."

Grant looked down at the bedclothes. "I've slept on worse," he observed.

She shot him a guardedly admiring glance. No matter what she threw at him, he took it in stride without complaint. She twirled around and marched back to the bedroom, where she dressed hurriedly.

When she came out, Grant had just finished preparing his bed for the night.

"I make a pretty good bed, if I say so myself," he said with feigned pride.

Leida tossed it a cursory glance. "It'll do."

Grant's eyes swept over her. "You look lovely."

"Thanks," she said curtly. She'd selected a deep red, lightweight dress with cap sleeves and a V-neckline. Her curly dark hair tumbled onto her shoulders and bounced when she walked. She wanted to look attractive, so she had taken extra pains to put on her makeup just right. She wanted Grant to desire her.

She'd already caved in to his apology, and in her heart, she'd almost completely forgiven him. But she wasn't going to let him know that yet. It was going to take time to heal the wounds—to restore trust between them.

Grant escorted her to his waiting car. When they'd located the restaurant district, he found a place to park. As they emerged from the sleek automobile, a small boy appeared as if from nowhere.

"Watch your car, *señor*?" the dark-haired child asked.

"Sure," Grant said affably. "Here." He handed the boy a handful of coins.

The child's eyes lighted up.

"Thanks, *señor*," he said.

"There'll be more for you when we return if you're still here and my car is all right. Okay?" He winked at the boy as if to seal their bargain.

"You can count on me, *señor*. Nobody will touch your car while Pepe is on the job."

"I'm counting on you, Pepe," Grant responded, tousling the child's hair.

Pepe smiled. Then his face took on a stern demeanor, a direct challenge to anyone to invade his protective territory around Grant's vehicle.

Leida was touched by Grant's kindness to the small boy. She wanted to slip her arm through his and tell him how impressed she was. Instead she walked along beside him, her hands to herself.

The atmosphere of the town was charming. Streetlights softly lit the adobe buildings with their old-world architecture. An elderly woman in a black shawl and faded dress shuffled along the street next to a young man who appeared to be her son. Young couples in American clothes entered and left eating establishments. The shops and many of the other buildings sported black grillwork protecting the windows and glass doors.

Grant pointed out a likely-looking restaurant. They entered and were seated at a cozy table where a waiter in a stiff tuxedo bowed politely and took their order in English.

When the man left, Grant chuckled. "I thought I might have to use my rusty high school Spanish. Fortunately, he could speak English."

"I've found most of the people who deal with the public can speak some English," Leida replied.

"That's how I've managed to get around. I don't speak Spanish at all."

When the waiter brought a basket of nachos—crisp tortilla chips—they both helped themselves. As she reached into the basket, her hand touched Grant's. A bolt of electricity shot through her. She hesitated and then snatched her hand away, self-consciously hiding it in her lap.

Later, when they had finished their chicken mole and *chalupas*, Leida put her hand on the table. Grant's hand settled gently on hers. She looked up into his liquid brown eyes, soft, warm eyes, loving eyes, questioning eyes, that silently asked her to allow this to be the first step toward reconciliation.

Leida's pulse pounded. Her heart begged her to leave her hand there, to luxuriate in Grant's caress. But her intellect told her not to give in. This man had hurt her too deeply. So she gingerly slid her hand out from under his.

The evening was somewhat strained. The closeness they'd once felt had been shattered. Putting the pieces back together was a fragile balancing act. Sometimes Leida thought it might work out between them. Other times she felt their fight had inflicted irreparable damage on their relationship.

When they'd finished, Grant excused himself to pay the bill. He was gone longer than she'd expected. When he returned to the table, he held out his hand to help her up. She glanced from his outstretched fingers to his face. He was smiling, his expression urging her to take his hand. Instead, she got up by herself and walked past him, tossing him a faint smile as she passed.

She longed to throw herself into Grant's arms. But the pain of their breakup was still too great. He was going to have to be patient with her, to give her time. If he couldn't do that, he didn't really care very much about her.

After dinner, Grant drove Leida around the city. They passed the square, where single young men and women performed the ritual of the *paseo*. Leida knew it was an accepted custom that protective parents brought their daughters to the square on certain evenings to be seen by eligible young men looking for female companionship. The girls walked slowly in one direction, shyly glancing at the boys, who walked in a circle in the opposite direction. When a boy saw a girl he wanted to talk to, he stopped, asked her name and chatted with her. The girl's parents looked the boy over. If they nodded their approval, the young lady could accept his invitation for an evening together. Well-chaperoned Mexican young women began a courtship by inviting the man home for their first date.

Leida realized how much easier it was in Mexico to know the truth about one's romantic interest. Had she met Grant under such circumstances, he'd have known all about her work from the beginning. There would have been no sudden shocking revelation. Could she really blame him for his behavior when he'd found out she was Alex Carter?

However, she'd tried to explain she hadn't set out to deceive him. But he wouldn't listen to her. If he hadn't been so hot-tempered, he could have spared them both a lot of anguish. She looked at him as they passed the square, at the set of his jaw, at the skillful way he negotiated the small, dusty streets and avoided the battered cars careering in and out of unmarked intersections. There was no question that she loved him, would always love him. But could she ever forget their terrible fight enough to tell him how she felt? Could she trust his love for her to be strong enough to last a lifetime?

Grant drove around aimlessly for a while. They talked about his campaign. Finally, Leida looked at her watch. "Don't you think we should be getting back?" she asked. "It's late."

Grant checked the time and nodded. "All right."

As they approached her neighborhood, she felt slightly nervous. Once inside her home, would Grant actually sleep on the couch? Was that bed-making routine of his just a ruse to throw her off guard? After all, she would be alone in the apartment with him. Would he respect her wishes? Worse, did she really want him to?

Maybe it had been a mistake to agree to let him spend the night under her roof. Perhaps she should insist he go to a motel.

They parked the car and walked toward her apartment. Inside the courtyard, Leida froze. Sitting outside her door were dozens of baskets of beautiful flowers—roses, carnations, daisies, lilies, huge chrysanthemums. The sight took her breath away. She realized Grant must have ordered them at the restaurant when he took so long paying the bill.

When she could speak, she said, "Oh, Grant, they're beautiful!"

"Just a small token of my love for you," he said.

"But there are so many!" she exclaimed.

"One flower for each apology I owe you," he said.

She felt a pang of regret for the way she was treating Grant. He was doing everything in his power to show her how sorry he was.

As soon as she opened her door, a little man came scurrying from the darkness and carried all the arrangements into her place, setting them on the tables, on the floor, beside her canvases. They filled her apartment. Just then Leida heard guitar music and singing.

She hurried to a window. Standing in the courtyard outside one of the arch-shaped windows of her apartment were five Mexican men wearing colorfully decorated sombreros and ornate shirts and trousers. They strummed guitars and sang Spanish love songs.

Leida bit her bottom lip and smiled. A tear came to her eyes. She loved it. She felt special, perhaps for the first time in her life.

She pulled up a cane-bottomed chair and sat just inside the window, enjoying the perfume of the flowers that filled her apartment and smiling with delight as the mariachi group played several tunes. Their voices blended together in beautiful harmony, the soft, haunting strains weaving their magic spell on Leida. All the while Grant stood beside her, looking at her with love shining in his eyes.

Doors and windows in the courtyard opened. Faces peered out. Mothers held children in their arms so they, too, could enjoy one of the aspects of their Mexican culture.

A serenade for one's sweetheart was a tradition in Mexico. Leida had never dreamed she would one day be the recipient of such a romantic custom.

When the mariachis were finished, they bowed slowly. Before they backed away, Leida said, "Wait. Please." She rushed over and broke off several red roses from one of the arrangements of flowers. She hurried back to the window. "Thank you," she said. "That was beautiful." She kissed each rose and tossed one to each of the musicians.

They caught the flowers, kissed them as if picking up the taste of her lips from its petals, held it out to her in tribute and bowed again. As they left, the other spectators retreated from their vantage points.

Grant moved closer to her, asking softly, "No rose for me?"

Leida stared at him, a knot in her throat making breathing difficult. She knew what he had in mind, but she wasn't ready—she still needed time. She handed him the last rose she had in her hand.

He took it. He glanced down at it, kissed it gently and stared steadily at her, the rose extended then to her.

She swallowed hard.

She looked at him, her lips quivering. Her pulse raced. Her hands felt cold. "It's time for bed," she said stiffly.

"I know." His tone held undercurrents that unsettled her.

He looked at her expectantly. His face was so close, the rose so near. She stared at the rose as if hypnotized.

Then she put her hands over the petals, gently pushed it and Grant's hand away from her and stepped back into the room.

"I hope you'll be comfortable on the couch," she said shakily.

Chapter Twelve

Once during the night, Leida was awakened from a sound sleep. She heard her door creak open and the whisper of soft footsteps across her room. Her heart began pounding. Lying very still, she peeped from under her eyelashes.

A bright, full moon was sending a shaft of silvery light through an open window. In the soft illumination she saw Grant beside her bed. She struggled to look natural in sleep, breathing slowly, her muscles limp. But inside she was a quivering mass of anxiety.

Grant was kneeling beside her, his eyes fixed on her. He just stared at her, his gaze roaming over the lines of her face as if memorizing them.

He remained in that position for some time, gazing at her, a tender smile on his lips.

Finally, he arose and moved quietly out of the room, closing the door behind him.

Leida let out a pent-up breath. Why did he come in here? He probably couldn't sleep. What if she had let him know she was awake? What would have happened?

She thought about that as she stared through the window at the big, romantic moon.

"Now," she muttered, "*I* can't sleep!"

"Good morning," Grant said cheerfully. Leida opened her gritty-feeling eyes to a breakfast tray swept ceremoniously onto her lap. "I hope madame had a good night."

"You're in a very cheerful mood this morning," she muttered.

"Why shouldn't I be? I'm with the woman I want. What kind of mood are you in?"

"I'll let you know after I've had some coffee." She looked down at the tray in her lap. "Somehow this seems familiar. Haven't I played this scene before?"

"Seems like you have." He smiled as he placed a napkin under her chin and tucked it into the top of her filmy nightgown. His fingers brushed her breast, bringing a stinging rush of sensation to her body. Had the touch been an accident? The wicked gleam in his eyes made her doubt it.

"Grant!" she scolded.

"All right, all right," he surrendered, drawing his hand away. "A man can't help looking—"

"You were about to touch," she pointed out.

Grant shrugged. "Well, maybe just a little."

"There's no such thing as touching just a little. Either you do or you don't."

He nodded. "Okay, I don't mind if I do."

"Grant Hunter!" she fumed. But the sparkle in her eyes betrayed her.

"Are you angry?" he asked, tilting his head.

"Of course I'm angry," she retorted. But not really, she thought. She was enjoying this game of making him keep his distance for a little while. How long she'd be able to keep it up, she didn't know. His nearness was melting her resolve.

"Are you mad because I tried to touch you? Or because I didn't?"

Leida narrowed her eyes. "Get out of here!" she ordered, tossing a pillow at him.

He laughed. "Only long enough to bring my own breakfast in here so I can eat with you."

Leida smiled as she glanced at the tray on her lap. Her "tray" was the bottom of a cardboard box Grant had scrounged from her closet. He'd taken pains to decorate it with a scattering of flowers around her plate of tortillas, refried beans and rice. She sniffed the tired aroma of the warmed-up leftovers. Oh, well, it was better than most of her breakfasts.

Grant appeared in the doorway with another cardboard box containing a plate of food. He smiled and joined her by sitting on the edge of her bed. He held up the plate of warmed-up leftovers.

"Is this what you've been eating for breakfast?" he asked incredulously. "I couldn't find a decent thing in the kitchen."

"Actually," she confessed, "I usually just have coffee for breakfast. My neighbor brings over food rather often. I stick it in the refrigerator and nibble on it now and then. Most of it I give to other people."

Grant took a mouthful of beans. "Not bad," he mused. "Beans for breakfast. I guess I could get used to that if I had to."

"Down here, beans are a staple. The people eat them for breakfast, lunch and dinner. I may never eat another one as long as I live."

"Well, if you don't eat something, you're not going to live long enough to eat any more beans," Grant observed. "You're much too skinny."

"Thanks a lot!"

"You'll thank me once I fatten you up a bit. You've been working too hard and not taking care of yourself. You need a few days for R and R."

"You're not about to fatten me up, Grant Hunter," Leida protested. "I like being thin."

"But you're so thin now that you don't look well." He gave her a piercing look. "I did some thinking last night," he continued.

Was that when you sneaked in my room? she thought cryptically.

"We're going to fly to Monterrey today and take in the sights. We'll make it a little vacation. There are some interesting places I'd like you to see."

"Anything worth painting?" she asked.

"Plenty. But there won't be time for that. However, we can pick up a camera. I'll take photographs of anything you like. You can paint it later."

"Hmm," Leida sighed. "All right, you've talked me into it. You know my weak spot, don't you?"

"I certainly hope so," Grant said with a grin.

The rest of the day was a flurry of activity. They drove back across the border, obtained tourist cards and Grant made a phone call that resulted in one of his company planes arriving to fly them to Monterrey.

When they landed in the colorful Mexican city, Grant rented a car for a drive up Chipinque Mesa, a beautiful plateau 1,373 meters above sea level. From the lookout they had a breathtaking view of the valley below. On the mesa was a modern restaurant with a huge tree growing through its center. Leida and Grant ate a late lunch and snapped photographs of the lush vegetation of the area.

Wherever they went, Grant expertly handled waiters, clerks and officials. The sight of the broad-shouldered, bronzed Texan, a head taller than most of the residents, commanded immediate attention. His resonant voice got quick results.

There was time for a quick drive to Canyon Huasteca for more scenic vistas. After dinner, they checked into a hotel, where Leida insisted they take separate rooms.

The next morning they drove to Rock Gorge to see its sheer, steep walls of sulfur rock and to make a tour of Garcia Caves. Leida kept Grant busy snapping pictures of everything that caught her eye.

That afternoon they drove out of town and up a paved mountain road toward Horsetail Falls. They arrived at the parking area on the mountain in time to take one of the last trips up the dirt trail to the base of the falls.

The trip had to be made on foot or on burro. When they rented one of the beasts of burden, Grant explained, "The young boys who lead the animals up the trail earn money to help their families. I believe in helping kids who are willing to work." Grant had made this trip before and was familiar with the procedure.

Leida smiled. By now it was the sort of attitude she expected from Grant. He wasn't at all the heartless monster the Austin newspaper had depicted in its editorials. She wished she could set editor Sam Daniels straight about Grant. But her former editor would never believe her.

Several people were mounting the small burros, settling onto the blanket across each animal's back for the bumpy ride up the one-and-a-half-kilometer path. Leida rode sidesaddle while Grant sat astride his animal.

The trip up the mountain trail was slow. The burros walked at a snail's pace past small trees, near little streams of water flowing down the hillside, over the rocky terrain. Leida's burro swayed from side to side and she was bounced and jostled by stride. But the ride was delightful. She especially enjoyed the conversation of the young boy who led her burro. She studied his face, his eyes bright with anticipation as he glanced over at her escort, Grant. The child could obviously spot a rich American.

She hoped she could capture that expectant expression on canvas. She had Grant snap several pictures of the boy, who posed proudly for the camera. However, the lens of the camera was not nearly as sensitive to the inner personality of its subject as was the paintbrush. Would she be able to reproduce that vibrant, excited gleam in the boy's eyes?

Grant's burro was led by an older boy who maintained a more stoic expression. He spoke little.

When the stream of people arrived at a flat plateau, everyone dismounted. Grant helped Leida slip off the burro. His lips brushed her hair causing her heart to beat harder.

There was an aura about this rustic scene that heightened her senses, that made her more aware of Grant's closeness.

The cool mountain air tinged with a hint of moisture invigorated Leida. She felt like running and dancing and throwing caution to the winds. The cool vegetation growing around them pulsated with life. She could hear the sound of rushing water, could almost smell the clean, clear aroma of a pristine mountain stream.

Grant took her hand and led her to a wooden platform and a series of steps that ascended to the falls. She liked the warm pressure of his hand. She smiled, her eyes glowing as she looked at him.

They climbed the steps with the others. By now, the crowd had diminished. Most visitors came earlier in the day, and down below, many of the burros had already been retired to their evening quarters to rest for the next day's work.

As they neared the falls, Leida was struck at how quiet everyone had become. Tourists climbed the steps

slowly, gazing in anticipation in the direction of the
sound. Then the giant waterfall came into view. It was
breathtaking. The white water roared over the brink
of a high, sheer cliff, crashing majestically in an end-
less accordion fan to the foot of the falls far below.
From there the water gushed into a river that snaked
through the mountain.

A fine spray settled on Leida as she cast her eyes up
at the top of the falls. Horsetail Falls. She understood the significance of the name. The swirling water began at a narrow edge of the ridge high above and
spread out wider as it hurtled down through space like
the sweep of a horse's tail.

The scene was gorgeous. The sun was dropping
slowly behind the edge of the mountain, sending a
cascade of rainbow colors streaming through the fine
spray that hovered over the top of the falls. The air
had grown cooler.

Grant snapped several photographs for Leida from
different angles. Then he stood next to her, admiring
the beauty.

"Are you glad we came?" he asked, slipping an arm
around Leida.

"I certainly am," she said emphatically. "This is
magnificent, Grant."

"There are many more things I want to show you,
Leida, scenes you'd love to paint. Places with a char-
acter all their own, in France, Italy, England, the Far
East."

His voice was filled with emotion. He was gazing at
her with a look that melted away the last fragments of
doubt. Her eyes were turned up to his. She looked at

this tall, brawny Texan who could speak with such eloquence, command a situation with his forceful presence and yet tenderly serve her breakfast on a tray made out of a piece of cardboard. Her eyes grew misty as her heart swelled with love. Forgotten were the weeks of heartbreak when she had determined to erase him from her mind.

Not taking his eyes off her, he reached in a pocket and took out a small, velvet box.

"Open it," he urged.

She stared wide-eyed at the box, turning it over in trembling fingers. "Grant," she whispered unsteadily. Then she looked at him through sudden tears. "You open it," she said, her mouth dry.

Grant smiled, took the box from her hand and lifted the lid. He turned it toward her. She gasped.

"Oh, Grant!" It was beautiful—the largest diamond she'd ever seen. With a brilliant flash, it caught the rays of the setting sun.

"Please say you'll accept it, Leida," Grant said huskily.

Tears sprang to her eyes. She couldn't speak for a moment. She nodded, her heart ready to explode with joy.

Grant slipped the solitaire on her finger. "Leida, oh, Leida, my darling," he murmured. He pulled her to him, showering her face with kisses.

"I love you, Grant, so much...so very, very much." So much, she thought, that it frightened her. She loved him with a total commitment. There was no turning back now.

Their lips met, their mouths hungry. His arms became steel bands. Her body strained against his eagerly, with an abandoned wantonness. There was no holding back. Desire became a burning force that throbbed in her veins, made her breasts ache with a desperate longing for his touch.

Then Grant stroked her hair tenderly, gazing deeply into her eyes. "Marry me, Leida." He held her as if she might disappear if he let her go.

"Yes, darling."

"Now. I don't want to take a chance on losing you again."

She pulled back. "Now?" she asked, disbelieving.

"Now," Grant affirmed. "Here in Mexico. Before you change your mind and run away again."

"I'm not going to run away again, you idiot!"

"I want to make sure of that. I want you now, as my wife. I want you tonight."

"I know," she whispered thickly. "And I want you." She laughed. "Okay, darling. We'll get married."

Grant sighed happily and pulled her closer again, planting a long kiss on her willing lips. He held her close, his hard, masculine body hinting of promises to come, promises that she hungered to have fulfilled.

She was in a mental fog on the trip down the mountain. She was too deliriously happy to notice the bumpy ride back to their rented car. She gazed at her engagement ring and then at Grant, wondering if this was all a dream.

It was late when Grant rousted out a Mexican official to perform their wedding ceremony. Leida signed some documents written in Spanish, said her vows to words she didn't understand as the official sleepily pronounced them man and wife in Spanish.

Then they were at the airport, taking off for the return trip to Texas. In the Lear jet, the trip took less than an hour. On the way, Grant radioed orders to have one of his cars sent to the airport. When they landed in Brownsville, a Lincoln Continental was waiting.

The morning sky was tinged with the first rays of dawn's light as they drove across the causeway to Padre Island. Only a few decades ago, the long, sandy strip stretching up the Texas coast like a golden scimitar had been a remote frontier inhabited only by a few fishermen and beachcombers and accessible only by boat. Then a modern causeway had linked the southern tip to the mainland. Now hotels and condominiums stretched along one of the finest swimming beaches in the United States.

"Grant, this is insane." Leida giggled, her head resting against his shoulder as he drove. "I don't have any kind of beachwear. All I have is the overnight bag I took with us to Monterrey."

"That's no problem. There are plenty of shops over here. We'll go shopping in the morning."

"Where are we staying?"

"I have a company condominium on the island."

The condo was luxurious. Grant carried her over the threshold. Gently, he laid her on a king-size bed and sat beside her. His hands clasped hers and brought her fingers to his lips. He kissed the tips tenderly, looking at her all the while. Her arms slipped around his neck.

She couldn't take her eyes from his. There was a depth of communication between their eyes beyond physical contact.

Then Grant unbuttoned the top of her blouse. As he did so, she unsnapped the waistband of her skirt. Fabric rustled, made a sliding noise and whispered onto the carpet. A creamy shoulder was bared, then another, and the companion to the skirt joined its partner on the floor near open-toed sandals that were kicked off of slender feet.

Grant's eyes swept over her. "You are so beautiful, Leida," he whispered huskily.

Then his fingers touched one shoulder, lifting a strap and pulling it down her arm. He performed the same task with the other shoulder. Then he bent down, his mouth seeking out the delicate curve of smooth skin.

Desire became a raging flame through her body, igniting a heat in her breasts that rose and fell with her gasping breath. "Oh, Grant," she sighed.

"Leida, I've longed so for this moment," he said hoarsely.

"Yes," she whispered. She cupped his face in her hands, gazing into his eyes. "Grant, I love you so much. I've not had a whole lot of love in my life. I've never been in love before—not like this. It's frightening, like a big, overpowering force that's been locked up inside me and now I don't have any control over it anymore. I want you terribly and I want to—to give you all of me. I want to make you happy."

"You will—you do—"

There was silence in the room except for Leida's soft exclamations as Grant's lips and caresses ignited fires all over her trembling body.

"You're everything I've ever wanted, Leida," he said huskily. "Thank heavens I didn't let you slip away from me."

She couldn't speak. There was only sensation and mounting waves of pleasure. Her throbbing breasts were flattened against his broad, muscular chest. She welcomed the contact of his bare flesh against hers. Her legs eagerly clasped the corded muscles of his thighs. There was nothing separating them now. Their bodies were entwined. She strained against him, and cried out when they became one.

"Grant, oh, Grant."

The rhythm of their lovemaking matched the pounding of the waves on the shore. Passion raged like a fire out of control, mounting higher and higher until it burst in a breathtaking culmination. Leida saw flashes of the fire behind her closed eyelids, heard her cry of ecstasy over the rush of blood in her ears.

They spent hours in rapturous love, exploring each other, cresting to the intoxicating heights of ecstasy, lying in each other's arms, dozing, waking to continue the highest expression of their desire for each other.

At noon the next day, they shopped for beachwear. Then Grant rented a jeep and announced that they were going to drive up the beach, away from civilization for a picnic. He shopped for picnic supplies, then away they went, driving on the smooth, hard-packed beach on the water's edge.

After a while, the beach became desolate and rough. To their right was the gulf, green rollers dissolving into frothy surf. To their left were the silent, mysterious sand dunes in clustered mounds and hillocks, fringed by waving sea oats. The beach here was wild, a desolate, sandy roadway littered with driftwood. Leida knew that many of the barnacle-encrusted logs had floated across the gulf from as far away as South and Central America. The smooth sand gave way to shell banks through which their jeep gamely plowed. "I can see why you need a four-wheel-drive vehicle here," Leida said, hanging on for dear life.

Grant nodded. "We're coming to the area known as Big Shell and the Devil's Elbow. That's a great area for beachcombing. All the currents of the gulf wash up there. You can find everything from pieces of wrecked ships to oil drums."

A few minutes later, he pulled up beside a gigantic driftwood log and parked. "This suit you?"

"Yes." A little shiver ran through her as she gazed around at the scene of desolate loneliness surrounding them. "I feel like we're on another planet."

"This is pretty remote," he agreed. "Except for an occasional fisherman, you might not see another living soul all day. Are you hungry?"

"Ravenous. All this fresh sea air has given me an appetite."

From the jeep he brought a folding picnic table, some pots and pans and a sack full of assorted vegetables and spices. "We're going to be beachcombers and get our dinner from the sea. Coquina stew. Ever have any?"

Leida shook her head. She watched as Grant gathered together a pile of driftwood and got a campfire going.

"Are you sure you know what you're doing?" she asked.

"Yes, but I'll need some help digging up the coquinas."

The tiny marine clams were swept onto the beach by each wave, hundreds of them tumbling over and over on the hard-packed sand at the water's edge. As the wave receded, leaving them stranded, they upended and burrowed quickly into the sand.

Grant got buckets from the jeep and they began digging handfuls of coquinas from the wet sand. The tiny mollusks were not much larger than a dime so quite a few were needed. They washed all traces of sand from them and dumped them into another large pot of water that Grant then set over the fire.

"They have to boil long enough to make a strong broth. Then we fry bacon until it's crisp, crumble that up and add it to the stew. Next we brown some onions in the bacon fat. After the coquinas are cooked, I'll pick some of the meat out of the shells and add that to to the broth."

That done, Grant cut up potatoes, celery, parsley, carrots, then added a diced fresh tomato, a can of tomato sauce and a little barley. Salt, pepper and a pinch of thyme provided the seasoning.

"All that has to cook another thirty minutes," Grant explained. "Then we add some milk to the stock and give it a last reheating."

"Grant, I'll collapse from hunger by then."

"Then here's something to tide you over."

From a picnic basket, he laid out a spread of hors d'oeuvres: crackers, dip, caviar.

Eventually Grant announced, "The coquina stew is done. Ready for a sample?"

She eyed it uncertainly. "You're the cook. Maybe you better try it first."

"Okay." He laughed. He dipped a spoon in the steaming pot and gave it a cautious taste. "Hey! Not half-bad."

Leida tried a spoonful. "Grant, it's delicious! How did you ever learn to make it?"

"My dad brought me to Padre Island on fishing trips when I was a kid. We went with an old fishing guide named Pete, who knew every inch of the island. That old guy could do marvelous things with a driftwood fire, a few pots and any kind of fish you'd bring him. He taught me how to make coquina stew. He said you'd never starve if you got lost on the island. You'd never die of thirst, either. Dig a few feet down anywhere and the hole will fill with fresh water. It's a little brackish, but drinkable."

Grant continued, lost in his memories. Leida sat quietly, wanting to hear more about Grant's childhood. "We'd sit around the campfire at night listening to the coyotes howl back in the sand dunes, while old Pete would spin yarn after yarn about shipwrecks, pirates and buried treasure. He showed me some pieces of eight he'd found, so I guess his stories weren't all fiction."

"That must have been a wonderful adventure for a boy," Leida exclaimed.

Grant nodded. "It was. I loved coming down here."

After the meal, Grant said, "Ready for a swim?"

Leida nodded. "That water looks inviting, so blue and clear."

"Lots of strong currents here and it drops off pretty fast," he warned. "We don't want to get out too far."

"Agreed! I've had enough near-drowning experiences for a lifetime."

Leida went to the jeep for her bathing suit. She looked around. "Should I go behind the dunes to change?"

"Why? There's nobody to see you except the sea gulls."

"All right, then." She unbuttoned her blouse, slipped it from her shoulders. Then she removed her shorts. She felt the sun and the wind on her body. It gave her an exhilarating feeling of freedom. Then she felt Grant's gaze, drinking in the sight of her. Goose bumps broke out all over her. She didn't hurry putting on the one-piece swimsuit. It was exciting, knowing Grant was looking at her, that the sight of her like this could enflame him with desire.

With a carefree laugh, she ran through the sand and plunged into the waves. She looked back to the beach, saw Grant dressed in white swimming trunks that were a contrast to the golden tan of his broad chest and strong legs. He loped down to the water as lithe as a jungle cat and dived in beside her.

They played in the waves, laughing like children on a holiday. Once, Leida felt the frightening tug of the undercurrent, but immediately, Grant had her in his arms and with a few powerful strokes, they were back in safe waters.

They stood close together, their arms around each other. Leida felt her heart beating hard against Grant's chest. She felt her bare legs rub against his. His hand slid down her back, searching the curves of her hips under her swimsuit. They looked into each other's eyes and knew what they wanted.

Without a word, Grant scooped her up and strode out of the water. He spread a blanket beside the big driftwood log.

"Grant, right here, out in the open?"

He smiled, his eyes growing smoky with hunger for her. "Afraid you'll scandalize the sea gulls?"

Desire flamed in her. She felt daring and abandoned. Without another word, she slipped the straps of her bathing suit down. Grant reached for her, tasting her quivering breasts. She dug her fingers in his hair with a soft moan.

With shaking fingers, she pushed the suit over her hips. It fell around her ankles.

Grant lifted her in his arms and gently placed her on the blanket.

The gulf breeze rustled the sea oats.

Above them a sea gull called.

Chapter Thirteen

The next three days passed in a golden haze.

Their nights were spent in rapturous love, exploring each other, cresting to the intoxicating heights of ecstasy, lying in each other's arms, dozing, then waking to continue. They walked on the beach at sunset, hand in hand, silently content to be together with the outside world far away. Time was an elusive phantom. All that mattered was their love, their sharing, their desire.

They rode into town and picked up a few art supplies. Grant dozed in the warmth of the late-afternoon sun while Leida painted scenes of their surroundings. Her work exhibited a new quality, a vitality that reflected her newfound happiness.

"Leida, you're a very talented artist," Grant said with pride. "I'm going to see to it that you have that art show."

"Oh, no, you won't," she protested. "That's something I'm going to do on my own. It wouldn't mean the same if you paid some gallery owner to show my work. I want my paintings to be displayed in a gallery that appreciates the merits of my ability."

"Have it your way," Grant conceded. He turned her in his arms and gave her a long, slow kiss.

The golden honeymoon days passed all too quickly. Then it was the morning they had to return to the harsh world of reality.

When Leida awoke that morning, she moved closer to Grant, snuggling her head on his shoulder, wanting to hold on to these final romantic moments.

She kissed him awake. Grant stirred sleepily. His arm tightened around her and he gave her a groggy smile. "Morning, sweetheart."

She caressed his stubbled cheek, as he glanced at the watch on his wrist and sighed. "Well, today it's back to the rat race, huh?"

She nodded. A wave of melancholy swept over her. "Let's not go back. Let's just stay here forever."

He chuckled. "Don't tempt me."

"I wish I could. I don't want to go back, Grant. Somehow I'm afraid." A strange chill made her shiver and snuggle closer to him. "Everything's so perfect here. I'm afraid when we leave, something bad will happen."

"Nonsense." He smiled. "What can happen?" he asked, then sighed. "Much as I'd like to stretch this out, I can't, Leida. I have a political race to run. And," he reminded her, "you have an art showing to arrange."

"I know," she said with a sense of resignation.

"Four weeks until the election," he muttered, shaking his head. "Boy, I'm going to have to really get busy. My campaign people are probably crawling the wall over the way I disappeared the past few days."

"Maybe I should have held out a little longer, kept you to myself." She sighed. "Selfish, huh?"

"You held out long enough," he growled. "You had me pretty worried in Mexico."

She sat up beside him. "Well, you had it coming," she said with a pout. Then the pout turned into a radiant smile. "But we made up for it these past three days, huh?"

He gazed up at her, at the sight of her tousled hair, her fresh young face. "We sure did," he said, nodding slowly.

He brought her hand to his lips, kissing it tenderly. He looked at the diamond on her ring finger. "Tell you what. Something to cheer you up. After the election, we'll have a big Texas wedding and I'll make an honest woman out of you."

She gave him a puzzled look. "What are you talking about?"

"That marriage ceremony in Monterrey. There's some question in the States about the legality of Mexican marriages.'' He grinned. "We might be living in sin.''

"Why, you rat!'' She hit him with a pillow.

He laughed. "All's fair in love and war.''

"It's liable to be war, Grant Hunter.''

He continued to regard her with an amused expression. "Isn't it a little bit titillating, being in bed with me and maybe we aren't really married?''

She flushed. "Maybe. But I want us to be married. Why do we have to wait until after the election? Can't we just go to a justice of the peace on this side of the border?''

"We could,'' he agreed. "But with the election so near and the race so close, we'd better be discreet about it until after November. As you know, my opponent is running a dirty race and there's a lot of mudslinging going on. His people would jump on any hint of personal scandal. The way I suddenly broke off my engagement to Alice Townsend to marry another woman could cost me enough votes to swing the election.''

She looked at him thoughtfully. "That sounds like your campaign manager, Clayton Brooks, talking.''

"You don't like him much, do you? Can't say I blame you, the way he tried to break us up. I'll be frank with you, Leida, I don't have a lot of use for the guy personally, myself. He's a ruthless little bastard. But he knows his business. If anybody can get me that election, he can.''

"It's really important to you, isn't it, Grant?" she said slowly. "Your political future means everything to you."

He agreed soberly. "Yes, it is very important to me, Leida. I really want to win that election."

She nodded thoughtfully. "Then I'll certainly do whatever I can to help."

He squeezed her hand. "That's my girl."

"What do you suggest we do?"

"I'm afraid you're not going to see a lot of me the next four weeks. I'm going to be running myself ragged all over my district, trying to keep in the public eye—making speeches, attending campaign rallies, filming TV spots. It would probably be a good idea to get you settled in a comfortable apartment somewhere."

"I can go back to Austin," she said slowly. "I might be able to get my old apartment back. I want some art dealers there to see my work. Maybe I can interest one of them in setting up a show."

She paused, tears coming into her eyes. "I'm going to miss you...."

"And I'm going to miss you," he said, his eyes growing intense. "But I'll be able to steal a night here and there to be with you. And after the election, we'll have a real Texas-style wedding and another honeymoon and we'll be together all the time."

"It sounds so wonderful," she said wistfully.

She felt his gaze roaming over her, warming her body. She knew what the look in his eyes meant and she felt her breasts grow full and her nipples harden as a flame of desire was suddenly aroused in her.

He reached up slowly, unbuttoning the front of her pajama top. It fell apart. She felt the heat of his concentrated gaze. He reached up and his hands caressing her quivering breasts made her gasp. His murmur was hoarse. "We don't have to leave for another hour—"

He slipped the pajama top from her shoulders, pulled her down to him and buried his face in the soft fragrance of her bosom. She felt the tickle of his morning stubble on her tender flesh and she shivered at the delicious sensation.

Under the covers, he was slipping her pajama bottoms from her hips. She reached for him, her hands exploring, eager in their stroking caress.

Then her thoughts were blotted out in a haze of mounting ecstasy.

After breakfast, Grant made a phone call that sent some of his men to Leida's apartment in Mexico to pack her belongings and transport them to Austin. Then she and Grant flew to Austin where she was able to rent her old apartment again. And the next thing she knew, he was gone.

Leida felt cold and empty inside. Her arms ached for Grant. Her first night alone left her feeling miserable and depressed. To fight the loneliness, she attempted to do some sketching. But even that didn't completely obliterate the empty sensation that haunted her.

Grant phoned her every night. She could hear the keyed-up tension in his voice and the fatigue. This race was taxing him to the limit. She was worried, but there was nothing she could do but sit helplessly on the sidelines.

When they'd been apart a week, Grant called as usual. "Hi, sweetheart," he said. "I just have a minute."

Leida's heart raced when she heard his voice. "I miss you," she said.

"I miss you, too. But I'm going to make up for lost time when I see you. Looks like I'm going to have a break this weekend. I'm flying to Austin late Saturday. Sunday morning, we'll fly to the family ranch. My folks want to meet you. Sound okay with you?"

Leida swallowed, feeling suddenly nervous. "Sure, that's okay. Grant?"

"Yes?"

"What . . . what if they don't like me?"

"Don't be silly. What's not to like?"

"But you come from a different world than mine, Grant. I've never been around people like your family. I've been poor all my life."

He laughed. "Leida, they're not snobs. They'll like you. Look, I've got to rush. Have to be at a PTA meeting in ten minutes. See you Saturday—"

His words did not reassure her. She was eager for his family to accept her, but would they? Perhaps they'd think of her as an interloper. After all, they'd expected Grant to marry Alice Townsend.

It was a little frightening to consider facing the Hunter clan. She'd be on display like a maverick animal being scrutinized to see if it could fit into the fold. She didn't relish the prospect. However, she knew that sooner or later she had to meet them.

That week Leida drove to the coast and spent a couple of days on the houseboat. Her waterfront quarters helped fill her with a sense of security and peace. She took long strolls on the beach and spent hours painting.

When she returned to Austin, Leida felt refreshed. She made the rounds, talking to the owners of local art galleries about an exhibit of her work. One showed a definite interest in her portfolio and asked to see larger works. She was delighted. She set up an appointment for the next week so the gallery owner could have a better look at her entire collection.

After leaving the gallery, Leida started to look forward to her time alone with Grant before he whisked her off to meet his family.

She'd gone to extra trouble to cook Grant a candlelight dinner. It hadn't been easy. She wasn't the domestic type at heart, but she wanted to please Grant, to show him how much she loved him. She'd spent considerable time poring over recipes, shopping for the necessary items she'd need to whip him up her best dinner, and fussing in the kitchen, starting plenty early in case she created a disaster and had to start over.

When Grant didn't arrive on time, she forced herself to be patient. Then he called and said he'd been held up. She hid her frustration. After she hung up, she wept over her meal, now hopelessly ruined from being kept warm too long.

It was late when Grant finally arrived. His appearance at her door set her heart fluttering, like an infatuated high school girl. In an instant she forgave him his tardiness.

She was concerned at how tired he looked. He seemed distracted. He took several phone calls while with her, leaving her to sit alone on the couch, staring at her fingernails and longing for his attention.

"I'm sorry," he apologized, after one of his calls. He joined her on the couch. "I know this campaign is hard on you. It won't always be like this, darling, I promise. I've been running all over the district trying to win votes. Campaigns get the most hectic as the election nears. In a few more weeks, this will all be over, and we can begin to lead a normal life."

Leida bowed her head. "I know." She felt guilty. Was she being selfish to resent the time Grant spent away from her? This campaign meant so much to him. He was the kind of politician the state needed. She had to be patient.

The evening was nothing like she had planned. She'd envisioned the two of them having a leisurely, intimate dinner, making plans for the future and making love. Instead, Grant picked at the dinner she'd worked so hard to prepare, spent most of the time on the phone and seemed harried and pressed for time. Once, he took her hand in his while he was talking to someone about a campaign billboard advertisement, but he soon had to leave her to herself to make some notes about his conversation.

At last, Grant swept her to bed, apologizing all the while for the interruptions. He was the consummate lover, taking her to planes of ecstasy. For a while she forgot the bitter ache of having to keep their love a secret and the frustrations of being ignored so much.

She'd hoped to spend more time in his arms. But afterward, he fell into an exhausted sleep. She lay awake in the dark, staring at the ceiling. She couldn't have been more disappointed.

The next morning, Leida awoke to an empty bed. Grant was already dressed and talking on the phone again. She'd hoped they'd have more time together. But that was not to be. He urged her to hurry getting dressed and then they drove off for the airport where they boarded Grant's jet for the trip to the Hunter ranch in West Texas.

When they landed on the private strip far behind the main house, they were met by a tall, thin man in an all-terrain vehicle who loaded their luggage and whisked them to the ranch house.

The ranch-style mansion sprawled over the landscape, taking up what seemed like acres of land. The white-frame-and-native-stone structure was meticulously kept, as were the grounds that surrounded it. Several expensive automobiles were parked in a large graveled area to the side.

Leida suddenly felt apprehensive and nervous. Butterflies fluttered in her stomach. Be natural, she tried to tell herself. Relax. She took a deep breath, steeled herself and clasped Grant's hand for comfort. He smiled reassuringly, then opened the car door and gave her a hug as she passed him.

"They'll love you," he murmured in her ear.

I hope so, she thought. Would they know how nervous she felt?

Leida and Grant entered the house and walked down a long hallway. The walls were of a knotty pine with smooth wood grain giving the feel of the great outdoors. Leida could hear a classical melody being played on a piano somewhere in another room. She felt ill at ease and a strong sense of being out of her element overwhelmed her.

They entered a huge room with great, rough-hewn beams supporting a high, cathedral ceiling. In the center was a large fireplace open on all four sides. On the walls were hunting trophy heads: a wild ram from a western Texas mountain range; rhinos, elk and water buffalo from Africa. In front of the couch was a bearskin with the animal's gaping mouth showing a line of white teeth. One wall was decorated with African spears and shields. On another was a great gun case with dozens of costly rifles.

At the far side of the room sat a handsome, distinguished man behind a large desk. From his strong resemblance to Grant, Leida knew instantly that he was Grant's father. He was engaged in an animated conversation with a fellow who stood in front of him. As soon as the senior Hunter saw Grant and Leida, he stopped in midsentence. His gaze swept over Leida.

Then he smiled, nodded a gesture of dismissal at the other man and strode toward Leida and Grant.

He was dressed in an open-necked dark shirt and dark trousers and gleaming, hand-tooled Western boots. "Grant," he said warmly. "We've been expecting you."

The two men shook hands. Then Carl Hunter directed his attention toward Leida as Grant introduced them.

"So this is the young woman you've been telling us about," Carl observed.

His voice was cordial, but his eyes were penetrating.

"How do you do?" Leida said. She didn't know whether to extend her hand or not. He solved the problem by taking her hand in his and giving it a warm squeeze. He was certainly being gracious enough on the surface. Then why couldn't she relax? Was she imagining the look of cool speculation in his eyes?

"It's a pleasure to meet you, my dear," Carl said, nodding, his manner courtly. She could see how Grant had acquired his genteel, old-fashioned Southern gallantry.

"Thank you," she replied.

Just then a tall, poised woman wearing a simple but expensive looking pant suit entered the room. There was an air of aristocratic elegance about her. On her fingers was a blinding array of diamonds. She had ash-blond hair, high cheekbones and brown eyes. Grant must have inherited his brown eyes from her. Leida thought that in her younger days, Grant's mother might have been a fashion model. There was a delicate yet determined quality about her.

"I thought I heard someone come in," she said, smiling. "Grant, darling." She kissed his cheek.

"Hi, Mother," Grant said, putting his arm around her. "We heard you playing when we came in." He introduced Leida to Katherine Hunter.

"It sounded lovely," Leida commented.

Katherine nodded slowly, glancing at Leida with a guarded look. "How do you do, my dear." She extended a hand of greeting.

The same gracious welcome. And the same undercurrent of cool appraisal, Leida thought. Would the reserve melt after they became better acquainted. She tried to tell herself that this man and woman were now her father-in-law and mother-in-law, but it didn't seem very real to her.

But what did she expect? Leida asked herself. The Hunters and the Townsends were lifelong friends. They had expected a marriage between their offspring. Now, for reasons beyond their comprehension, at the most crucial point of his political campaign, Grant had suddenly changed his mind and married a stranger, a woman whom they knew nothing about. She was going to have to give them time to get used to the idea that she, not Alice Townsend, was their daughter-in-law. It was only natural that they would be cool to her. However, they were too well-bred to be blatantly rude or to appear shocked.

Katherine turned to Grant. "You had a phone call just before you arrived," she said. "Clayton Brooks. He said it was important."

"Of course," Grant replied. "Excuse me, darling," he said. "You don't mind if I leave you a moment, do you?"

Leida felt a touch of desperation. Of course she minded. But what could she say?

She smiled weakly. "Of course not," she replied. She wanted to say "darling," but she couldn't sound so intimate in front of Grant's parents.

Grant strode out of the room. Leida experienced a sinking feeling in her stomach. For a moment no one said anything. The Hunters stared at her. She felt something like a laboratory specimen under a microscope. Then Carl spoke. "Won't you sit down?" he offered.

Leida nodded. "Thank you." As she walked toward the couch, she told herself that she was being ridiculous. She had every right to marry Grant. He loved her. While she hoped for the approval of his parents, their blessing was not essential to their happiness. If they liked her and eventually accepted her, fine. If not, it wouldn't be because she didn't try to be congenial. Any animosity would have to come from them.

Leida settled uneasily on the couch. She bit her bottom lip. What would they talk about in Grant's absence?

She struggled for some topic to break the awkward silence. "That—that was a Chopin nocturne you were playing, wasn't it?"

Katherine Hunter looked surprised. "Why, yes. Do you know music?"

"I'm not a musician, but I have a smattering of knowledge of the classics."

"I see. Would you care for some coffee?" Katherine asked.

"Thank you, yes," Leida replied.

Carl strode to the far wall and pushed a button on the intercom to order coffee.

Meanwhile, Leida sat uncomfortably on the couch, staring at Katherine, whose eyes signaled a certain caution that unnerved Leida. While the older woman was outwardly pleasant enough, she had a guarded air about her.

There was another moment of silence, then Katherine said, "Grant tells me the two of you were married in Mexico."

Leida swallowed and nodded.

Katherine's smile didn't reach her eyes. "It was such a surprise. We had no idea..." Her voice trailed off. Then she said, "Grant can be rather impulsive sometimes. It sounds as if you two were in quite a hurry."

Leida frowned. Had she only imagined the implication in Katherine's words? No, I'm not pregnant, Leida felt like retorting. And Grant did not marry me on an impulse. He loves me. Then she told herself she was being too sensitive, too much on edge. Instead she replied, "Mexico is very romantic."

"Yes," Katherine nodded slowly. Whatever she was thinking or feeling was well hidden behind her poised, aristocratic features.

Carl rejoined them and took control of the conversation. "We're very glad Grant brought you to meet us, my dear," he said, bowing slightly as he took a seat opposite her. "We want you to get to know the family, to...understand us."

"Thank you," Leida replied, not knowing what else to say.

Leida sighed with relief when Grant appeared in the doorway. Behind him came a small woman carrying a tray laden with a silver coffee urn and cups and saucers.

"Leida, I'm sorry," Grant said with a frown. "Something urgent has come up. I'm going to have to leave shortly after lunch and be gone overnight. I'll be back early in the morning. You don't mind, do you?"

She shot Grant a desperate look. *Mind?* Of course she minded! She didn't want to be left alone with his parents. But how could she tell Grant that? She was certainly capable of taking care of herself, whether she'd enjoy the experience or not.

Leida shook her head, but her voice refused to lie.

Grant patted her hand.

The conversation turned to the election. Grant outlined the strategy Clayton Brooks planned to implement during the last weeks of the campaign. There were to be a media blitz, direct mail appeal, a heavy schedule of speeches, a door-to-door hand-shaking campaign in one particularly crucial area and a televised debate. Grant's time was booked almost solid until after the November general election.

During lunch, Leida felt like an outsider. Grant and Carl discussed politics like old hands who understood all the subtle nuances of the system. They tossed about percentages and demographic statistics and calculated Grant's chances for success depending on various scenarios that Brooks had proposed.

It was obvious to Leida that Carl Hunter relished this campaign strategy. He appeared to be vicariously living Grant's role in the political race.

Leida sat in the elaborate dining room with its large oak table, sideboard and expensive paintings on the wall and picked at her food.

Katherine, too, was absorbed in the political conversation. Every now and then Grant explained something to Leida. She smiled, nodded and then withdrew.

Finally, lunch was over and Grant hurried away. Leida felt terribly alone. Carl turned his attention to her.

"Well, my dear," he said, "with Grant gone, I'm sure you feel somewhat awkward with us. I'd like to put you at ease. Let me take you on a tour of the place, tell you something about the Hunters, give you some insight into the makeup of the family. I think it's important that we understand each other, don't you?"

"Yes, that would be fine," Leida replied.

Carl escorted Leida out the rear of the house and to the airstrip, where a metal hangar housed two Lear jets and a small prop plane. Mechanics were busy, wheeling the small craft out onto the runway.

"I don't want you to feel nervous about flying with me, Leida," Carl said, chuckling. "I flew with the navy in World War II. I've logged more hours in the air than a lot of commercial airline pilots."

They climbed into the small plane. Hunter checked the instrument panel, then pressed the starter. The prop made a few slow revolutions, the engine caught with a popping roar, and soon they were rumbling down the runway, picking up speed. The sudden upward lurch of the plane indicated when they were airborne. The senior Hunter's smooth, experienced handling of the controls quickly erased any uneasiness Leida had about flying in a small plane.

Next to the King ranch in South Texas, the Hunters had one of the largest single ranches in the state. They flew over thousands of acres. There were waterholding tanks, hundreds of miles of fences, streams, barns and hunting blinds. And there were oil wells. It was breathtaking.

"It's very beautiful," Leida commented. "Rustic, primitive, savage and yet settled."

Over the drone of the small plane's engine, Carl said, "As far as you can see to the horizon is Hunter rangeland. The Bar-H. It's been Hunter land for three generations. My grandfather fought Indians on this land and took part in the cattle drives to Kansas City. He built the ranch, buying land and more land until, before he died, he could ride all day and never leave his own land.

"This is where Grant grew up," Carl continued. "He worked hard as a youth. He never took what he had for granted. He loves this land the way we do."

This was all on such a grand scale, Leida had difficulty comprehending the vastness of what she was seeing. She felt strangely out of touch with reality. What was a girl who grew up on the wrong side of the tracks doing here, a member of one of the richest families in Texas?

"Grant has an important heritage in this state," Carl went on. "Since the day he was born, I've had but one dream and that is to one day see him in the governor's seat."

The intensity in Carl Hunter's voice took Leida by surprise. She glanced his way and saw the burning fire in his eyes. The big, rugged man radiated power. Leida suspected he might be dangerous if crossed. Under his genteel, courteous exterior, she sensed a burning lust for political power that he hoped to realize through Grant's career. It made her shiver.

There was a moment of silence. Then Leida said, "You're very ambitious for Grant."

"Yes, I am. He has great potential. I'd do anything to see him reach his goal."

Leida bit her lip. "Mr. Hunter, I know how you must feel about me—that I'm an interloper. That I'm a threat to Grant's winning this election."

The elder Hunter looked at her for a moment, then back at the vista below them. His expression was serious. "Yes, Leida, my dear, I am concerned. Deeply concerned. I'm worried, not only for Grant's sake, but yours, too. You seem to be a decent, sweet young woman. I'm worried that everyone involved could be hurt by this impetuous marriage. Grant could lose the election and you might have your heart broken.''

"I don't understand. I love Grant—''

"Yes, I'm sure you do. I don't question that for a moment. But Grant has known you such a short time. I am worried that the two of you were caught up in a romantic infatuation and acted rashly.''

"It's more than that! I love Grant. I plan to spend the rest of my life with him, trying to make him happy—''

"I hope Grant has the same commitment.''

She felt a sudden chill. "What do you mean by that?''

"What I said before. Grant can act impulsively at times, letting his emotions rule his better judgment. When he sees a challenge, he goes after it tooth and nail, the consequences be damned. In matters of the heart, one can be very foolish. I sincerely hope for everyone involved that it's going to work out for the two of you.''

Do you really? Leida wondered. I think what you really wish is that I'd somehow vanish into thin air like a bad dream!

When they returned to the Bar-H landing strip, Carl explained that he had some matters to attend to and he gave orders for one of the men at the hangar to drive Leida back to the main house.

As she walked into the large main room she heard voices. Katherine Hunter was having a conversation with another woman. They were seated on the large couch. Katherine looked up. "Oh, Leida. I didn't expect you back so soon. Did you have an enjoyable flight?"

"It was very interesting."

The other woman turned to face Leida. She was young, blond, very attractive. For a moment, Leida looked at her blankly. Then recognition struck her with a disturbing impact.

She was vaguely conscious of Katherine's voice. "Leida, I'd like you to meet Alice Townsend."

For a moment, Leida was too stunned to speak. What was Grant's ex-fiancée doing here?

As if answering her unspoken question, Katherine said, "The Townsends are our neighbors. Alice dropped by for a moment."

"How do you do," Alice Townsend said, arising from the couch. Her voice was formal, and the expression in her green eyes was cold, appraising. She was holding a drink in one hand and she made no attempt to put the glass down to shake hands, for which Leida was relieved.

Leida saw that Alice Townsend was even lovelier than the pictures she'd seen of her in the society pages. Her features were composed, her bearing regal. She had a flawless complexion, crowned by blond hair styled to flatter the oval shape of her face. Her voice was softly modulated, each syllable carefully pro-nounced. It was easy to understand why everyone thought Alice would be the perfect wife to further Grant's political career.

The discussion with Grant's father during the plane ride had left Leida with a headache. The last thing she needed was a confrontation with Grant's ex-fiancée. She was planning on telling her mother-in-law that she was feeling fatigued and wished to rest when Katherine interrupted. "Please excuse me for a few minutes. I have to discuss our dinner menu with the cook."

Much to Leida's dismay, Katherine walked out of the room leaving Leida alone with Alice. "Please sit down," Alice said, gesturing toward the couch. "Would you care for a drink?"

"No, thank you."

Leida sat stiffly on the edge of the couch. Alice took her place at the other end of the couch, curling her legs up under her so that she could face Leida. She leaned forward to put her drink on the coffee table, then settled back. Again her green eyes gave Leida a studied appraisal. "So, fate has brought us together," she murmured.

Fate? Leida was beginning to wonder if fate had anything to do with it. First there was the emergency that needed Grant's attention. Then the airplane ride with Grant's father during which he let her know what he thought about Grant marrying her. And now Alice "just happened" to drop by. This situation looked as if it had been arranged by Clayton Brooks and Grant's parents rather than by any design of fate.

Alice took a cork-tipped cigarette from a gold case. "Do you mind, terribly?"

Leida shrugged noncommittally.

Alice touched the flame from the gold lighter to her cigarette, inhaled deeply, then nervously snapped her lighter closed and dropped it in her purse. She looked down at the cigarette in her hand. "So Grant persisted until he won the game."

Leida frowned. "I don't know what you mean."

Alice's lips curved into a cold smile. "I mean you, Leida. Grant could never stand to lose at anything. In college, he was the star fullback who made the touchdowns. In business, it's Grant who makes the winning deals. In politics he's never lost a race, at least not so far. You presented a challenge that he just couldn't resist. How does the saying go? He chased you until you caught him."

Leida flushed angrily. "I think what I'm hearing is a classic case of sour grapes. It happens that Grant loves me and I love him. I'm sure you know that we're married."

"Oh, yes, that quick Mexican thing. Not entirely legal in the States, is it?"

Leida was growing angrier by the minute. Her head was pounding. "As soon as the election is over, we're going to have a wedding here in the States."

Alice raised an eyebrow as a cynical smile twisted her lips. "Are you quite certain of that?"

"Of course I am!" Leida jumped up furiously. "I don't have to sit here and listen to any more of this!"

"It might be better for you if you did," Alice said quietly. "You could save yourself some additional heartbreak." She arose and placed cool fingers on

Leida's arm. "There's really no reason for us to be enemies. I don't have anything against you, Leida. You're just a nice woman who got swept off her feet by the Hunter charm. This is not the first time that's happened. It's Grant who should be blamed." She sighed. "But I forgive him. That's just the way he is. A leopard doesn't change his spots. I've known Grant all my life, so believe me, I know what I'm talking about."

"No, I don't believe you!" Leida exclaimed. "Why should I? You're obviously jealous because I got Grant and you didn't. It's that simple."

Again Alice's lips moved in a cynical smile. "No, I'm afraid it isn't that simple." She picked up her drink and resumed her seat on the couch. She swirled the glass and the ice tinkled softly. She didn't take her eyes off Leida the entire time. "So Grant has convinced you that he's going to legalize that quickie Mexican marriage." She shook her head. "Grant can talk just about anybody into believing anything. You look like an intelligent woman. Do you really think a man with Grant's political aspirations would publicly marry someone with your background?"

Leida felt as if the breath had been knocked out of her. Her legs became weak, forcing her to sit on the couch again. "What are you talking about?"

"I know all about you, Leida. I know your real name is Wilson. You're from the wrong side of the tracks and you had a child out of wedlock—a child that you abandoned—"

The blood drained from Leida's face. "That's not true! What right do you have to delve into my private life? What kind of people are you, anyway?"

"I didn't investigate you, Carl did. When he found out that Grant was getting serious over you, he had the campaign manager, Clayton Brooks, run a check. As for your other question, what kind of people are we? The answer to that is that we're very powerful, very ambitious people. When you became involved with Grant Hunter, you starting playing in the big leagues. Carl Hunter is not going to stand by and see Grant's political future go up in smoke."

Tears were trickling down Leida's cheeks. "You've got it all twisted. My twin sister, Kara, had the child. She was sweet and good, a victim of circumstances. People in town often got us mixed up because we looked so much alike—"

Alice shrugged. "I believe you. But that doesn't mean anything. If the scandal sheets get hold of the story, they'll believe the gossips back in your home-town who think the worst of you."

Leida felt drained. The happiness she had known with Grant the past weeks was turning to ashes. Fighting back tears, she said dully, "Why are you so eager to turn Grant against me? If he's as selfish and ruthless as you make him out to be, why would you want him?"

"Good question. I suppose it's because I'm cut from the same kind of cloth. I'm just as ambitious and ruthless as any of the Hunters. Grant was supposed to marry me. I've planned my life that way. I want to be

Mrs. Grant Hunter when he becomes governor one day. I want to go to Washington as his wife when he becomes a senator from this state. Who knows...I might even become First Lady one day."

Leida shook her head slowly. "You are mistaken if you think I'm going to give up Grant just because of what you've told me today."

"Oh, you don't have to give him up," Alice said. "You never had him, Leida. Grant is going to give you up. You *were* a challenge to him. He's never had a woman walk out on him and disappear the way you did. That was a very smart move on your part. It aroused the hunting instinct in him. He was determined to find you. That's really what it was all about—a conquest. He'll keep you dangling a while longer, a convenient sort of mistress, and then when he's tired of you, he'll simply dump you. With his financial clout and legal know-how, getting that questionable Mexican marriage annulled will be a snap."

"You're saying all this out of jealousy!"

"Yes, I'm jealous," Alice admitted. "Grant is my man and I intend to fight for him. I'd be good for Grant. We were made for each other. We have the same backgrounds. My family could do a lot for Grant's political future. What can you do for him with your background, Leida? You can be sure the tabloids will make the most of your teenage reputation and the scandal in your hometown if Grant were to make your marriage public. But don't worry—he won't. He has too much political savvy for that. Grant is going to take what he wants from you and when his male ego is satisfied, he'll drop you. It won't be easy, but I'll swallow my pride and patch things up with him. That's how it's going to be. You might as well face the truth, Leida."

Leida felt as if her insides were being wrenched apart. "I don't believe all that for one minute!"

"I don't expect you to." Alice raised her chin with a look of challenge. "Go to Grant right now. Call his bluff. Demand a marriage ceremony here in the United States. Watch him run for cover."

Leida rose. Her head was splitting when she left the room and she went to the guest room to lie down.

She did not join the Hunters for dinner that evening. She spent a tortured night in the guest room, not wanting to believe Alice and yet torn with doubts.

The next morning, Katherine tapped on Leida's door and gave her the message that Grant had phoned. He'd said that he was going to be tied up the entire weekend and asked his father to have Leida flown back to Austin in one of the family's private jet planes.

Grant's father accompanied her. On the flight back to Austin he added to Leida's growing emotional confusion. "Grant still has a few wild oats to sow," the elder Hunter said. "I'm sorry you had to be hurt, my dear. You are an attractive, intelligent person. But I'm afraid my son has taken advantage of you. If there is anything I can do to make it easier for you, please don't hesitate to ask. I understand you are an inspiring artist. Perhaps you'd accept a year's art training in Europe by the finest teachers?"

He's trying to buy me off! Leida thought furiously. She didn't even reply. She turned her back to him, staring out the window at the scenery below.

Chapter Fourteen

I'm sorry, ma'am," the receptionist at Hunter campaign headquarters said. "I'm not sure where the senator is this morning. He's dashing around his district on an eleventh-hour, whirlwind of speech-making. If you'll hold on, please, I'll see what I can find out about his schedule."

Nervously Leida twisted the engagement ring on her finger while she cradled the phone receiver against her shoulder.

After returning from the Hunter ranch yesterday, Leida spent a lonely day in her Austin apartment, wrestling with her emotions. Her mood swung from anger to despair. For a while she would have herself convinced that she should view everything Alice said as the words of a desperate, jealous woman and dismiss them. But then doubt would creep back like a dark, ugly cloud.

She tried to recall everything Grant had said and done after he found her in Mexico. She remembered that she had been a little hurt when he asked that they keep their marriage quiet until after the election, but at the time, his explanation had satisfied her. She hadn't wanted to do anything that might harm his chance for reelection.

But now Alice and Grant's father had planted ugly seeds of doubt. If there was any question about the legality of the Mexican marriage Grant should have been willing to correct it right away with another ceremony on this side of the border. A part of her, wanting to defend him, argued that he just wanted to wait until after the election so they could make it a public ceremony, inviting all their friends. Once the present senatorial race had been decided, Grant wouldn't be so worried about media gossip over the way he'd jilted Alice Townsend to marry Leida. That would probably all die down and be forgotten in the next four years if he won the race. And if he lost, it wouldn't matter one way or the other.

But then Leida thought about the fact that Grant's father had dug up all the unpleasant hometown prejudice and gossip about Leida's past. She was quite certain that Alice would make sure the information reached Grant. Would he want to stay married to a woman who might be such a liability to his future public image?

Ever since returning to Austin from the Hunter ranch, Leida had been trying to locate Grant. It had been a frustrating twenty-four hours. He hadn't called her, hadn't returned her calls. His elusiveness only added to the uncertainty that Alice Townsend had awakened.

Alice's words still burned in Leida's mind. They were brutal words, biting words, words that begged to be disproved.

Could Alice possibly be right? Was Grant just using Leida? Had she been no more than a challenge his masculine ego couldn't resist? Was that all there was to their relationship?

As the wretched hours dragged by, her doubt began to grow. She began to question if she really knew Grant. Could she have been so terribly wrong about him?

The voice from his campaign headquarters came back on the line. "As near as we can determine, Senator Hunter is somewhere between cities on his speaking tour. We should have his whereabouts later on today if you'd care to call back."

Leida spent the rest of that day calling campaign headquarters, trying to track down Clayton Brooks, checking with various political groups to determine if Grant was scheduled to speak to them. All the while she felt her doubts and fears growing.

It wasn't until early on Tuesday, the following morning, that his campaign office had an updated itinerary on Grant and was able to give her his exact location during the day. She hurriedly scribbled the

information on a pad and immediately called the hotel in West Texas where Grant had a reservation.

"Yes, Senator Hunter is registered here," the clerk
confirmed when Leida called. "However, he's out of
the hotel and is not expected back until late tonight."

"But I have to talk to him," Leida protested.

"I'll be glad to take a message," the clerk said.

While Leida was speaking to the clerk, she realized
that she had to see Grant in person. Her doubts and
anguish would not be resolved by a simple phone
conversation. She could drive to the town where Grant
was speaking in two hours. If she hurried, she could
make it by noon, when Grant was scheduled to speak
to a luncheon group.

In a fit of desperation, she made up her mind to go.
She set out on the road and headed west, all the while
torturing herself with memories of her disastrous visit
to the Hunter ranch.

Several times she almost turned around and drove
back home. But a steely determination drove her on.
She had to know the truth.

Alice Townsend and Carl Hunter knew Grant much
better than she did. They might have been telling her
the truth. At first she'd refused to believe them. Alice
was obviously motivated by jealousy. However, Grant
had been so elusive lately, her doubts about him were
growing by the minute. The reason he gave for not le-
galizing the Mexican wedding with another ceremony
here in the States was beginning to sound flimsy. There
was only one way to find out. Confront Grant and in-

sist they legalize the Mexican marriage at once. If he really loved her, he'd agree.

When she arrived in the small town where Grant was scheduled to speak, she headed down the dusty main street and parked in front of the town meeting hall. The parking area was filled with cars, pickups and all-terrain vehicles. The smell of barbecuing beef was in the air. Leida got out of her car and took a deep breath of the cool, dry autumn air.

She quaked inside. Was she making a mistake? Was she about to wreck the one thing in her life that really mattered, her love for Grant Hunter? When she confronted him, would he send her packing, confirming that he'd never really loved her at all?

She hesitated. Did she really want to know the truth? She thought about that a moment. Yes, she had to know. There was no way she could continue their relationship otherwise.

Summoning all the determination she could muster, she strode toward the long, wooden building with its double screen doors. She pushed through them and surveyed the room. It was crowded with people seated on folding chairs stretched out in long rows. At the front of the room was a speaker's stand with a microphone. Near the front was a group of people Leida recognized instantly as the press.

She made her way down one side of the room and located a series of smaller rooms adjoining. As she stepped into one, she heard the deep tones of masculine voices through a door leading into an another room. Leida hesitated, her heart pounding. Then she opened the door and walked through. Clayton Brooks and three other men were engaged in an animated discussion. They stopped talking and looked at her with surprised expressions.

Leida directed her words to Clayton Brooks. "I need to see Grant."

Brooks murmured something to the other men and crossed to where she was standing. "Grant can't see you right now. He's about to make a speech."

Leida made no pretense of how she felt about the campaign manager. After the way he had spied on her and tried to turn Grant against her, she despised him. The expression in his small eyes made it clear the feeling was mutual.

"I have to talk to him," she said coldly. "It will only take a second."

"He's making some last-minute changes in his speech. I can't disturb him at a time like this," Clayton replied impatiently.

"But I've been trying to reach him for two days."

"I know. He's gotten your messages."

"What do you mean, he's gotten my messages? Why hasn't he returned my calls?"

Clayton shrugged. "How should I know? All I can tell you is that he was notified you'd called. Maybe he's too busy to talk to you."

Was Clayton telling the truth? If he was, it really hurt. Surely Grant would have found time to return her calls.

"Will he have time to talk to me after he makes his speech?" she asked.

"We're on a helluva tight schedule today," Clayton said, his tone impatient again. "As soon as he finishes speaking here, we have to whisk him to a rally two hundred miles from here. What's so all-fired important you have to talk to him today? Can't it wait until next weekend?"

Leida felt the dark shadow of depression mingling with her anger. She had been in a dismal emotional state ever since her talk with Alice Townsend on Sunday. Now the situation was growing more hopeless.

As she was standing there, immobilized by indecision, Grant suddenly appeared from another room. He was holding a sheaf of papers in one hand. Several men were around him, talking earnestly.

When he caught sight of her a look of astonishment crossed his face. "Leida!" He strode up to her. "What is it? Is something wrong?"

She hesitated. The other men in the room were staring at them. Suddenly she felt utterly foolish. How could she possibly discuss anything personal with Grant at a time like this? What had possessed her to drive here? She'd been too upset to think clearly. She should have known that it would be next to impossible to have any private moments with Grant.

"I—I just thought I'd surprise you," she stammered lamely. "I came to hear your speech."

"That's great," he said, looking at her with a puzzled expression. He glanced at his watch. "They're going to introduce me in a few minutes. Can we talk later?"

"Clayton says you have to hurry on to a rally."

Grant nodded. "Yes, that's true. But I'll have a few minutes—"

From the banquet room came the sound of applause. The campaign manager touched Grant's arm. "It's time. Bad public relations to keep them waiting."

Grant nodded. Again he gave Leida a puzzled look. "See you after the speech—"

"Yes," she said.

Grant left and Leida walked blindly out of the room. She found a seat near the back of the large banquet room. She was vaguely aware that a speaker introduced Grant to the group. She heard applause and he began his speech, but she was too preoccupied with her inner turmoil to be very attentive.

Grant spoke for thirty minutes. When the meeting ended, he left the speaker's stand and was immediately surrounded by people.

With a feeling of helpless frustration, Leida stared at the crowd around him. There was no way she would be able to speak to him in private. She rose and walked out of the building. Near the entrance were several long, black Lincoln Continentals, their motors running. They were waiting to whisk Grant and his entourage to his next engagement.

"I give up," Leida sighed. She walked around the Lincolns to her own little car, unlocked the door and slid behind the wheel.

"Leida!"

She glanced up at the sound of her name. To her surprise, she saw Grant detach himself from a group of men who had emerged from the doorway of the building and hurry toward her. She unlocked the door on the passenger side of her car and he slid in beside her. "I thought you were going to wait to talk to me after the speech."

"You were surrounded. There was no way I could get close to you."

"Sorry about that. What did you think of the speech?"

"It was fine," she murmured. No point in telling him she hadn't heard a word.

Grant was looking at her with a searching expression. "Leida, what's wrong? I know you didn't drive all these miles just to hear me give a speech."

Her mouth was dry. "There was something I wanted to ask you."

"Yes?"

She struggled to find the right words. "Grant, do you love me?"

He looked baffled. "Of course I love you, Leida."

Words like that were easy to say. Did he really mean them? Until two days ago, she had believed him completely. But not now. She drew a deep breath, not sure she wanted to ask the next question, not sure if she wanted to hear his answer. "Grant...could we get married right away?"

For a moment he looked too surprised to answer. Then he said, "But we are married, Leida!"

"Yes, I know. The Mexican marriage. I mean a real marriage, here in the States—one where there's no question about its legality."

Grant frowned, looking perplexed. "We've talked about this, Leida. I already told you, we'll get married after the election. We'll have a big ceremony, invite all our friends."

"I don't care about a big ceremony. It could be a justice of the peace—"

Grant shook his head slowly. "Leida, we've been over all of this. You know my chances of reelection are hanging by a thread. We agreed to keep our marriage quiet until after the election to avoid any last-minute gossip and—"

There was a loud tap against the car window on Grant's side. Leida saw Clayton Brooks staring at them. Grant rolled down the window.

"Grant, if we don't leave right now, we're going to be late and blow the rally."

"Yeah, be right there." Grant gave Leida a harried look. "I'm sorry, honey, I have to run."

Leida tried to hold back her tears. "Grant, it's important to me for us to get married—"

"I know. And we will. But not until after the election." He leaned over to give her a quick, parting kiss. "Now I have to run—"

Leida watched him hurry to the waiting cars. They pulled out of the parking lot in a flurry of dust. She sat there a while longer, her eyes smarting with tears. "Well, I guess I got my answer," she said bitterly.

Nothing had been solved by her impetuous trip to see Grant. When she got back to Austin, she paced the confines of her apartment, feeling lost and lonely. It became impossible to spend another minute in Austin. She threw some beachwear in a suitcase, locked up the apartment and headed for the coast.

When she reached the gulf coast, she got the mast and sail out of her houseboat and rigged up her little sailboat. Handling the mast brought back the heart-wrenching memory of the time Grant had purchased it for her.

From her boat she waved to her neighbor, Dora, and sailed out of the cove, setting her course for the open gulf. It was a sunny late afternoon, with the damp chill of late October in the air but no storm clouds on the horizon. Wrapped in a warm jacket, she settled back, welcoming the easy swells of the gulf. Her vision was on the distant horizon.

She wanted to forget everything and tried to will her mind a blank, but the memories of the past weeks were too strong. The scenes played over and over in her mind: the night she was pulled from the water to safety by a pair of strong arms, the stunned surprise of seeing Grant walk into the infirmary on the oil rig and realizing who he was, the recuperation at his beach house and the first thrill of her awakening attraction to him.

The bittersweet memories persisted...memories of the glamorous courtship when they had jetted around the country for intimate dinners. They had grown so close to each other so fast. And then there had been the agonizing separation when she fled to Mexico, and how, with a romantic flair, Grant had found her and swept her off her feet. The intoxicating honeymoon had been the highest peak of her life—lying in Grant's arms, foolishly believing he loved her and they had a real marriage.

Had all the dreams turned to ashes? What a trusting, naive fool she had been, she thought bitterly.

She was so lost in her thoughts that she was unaware of the time and how far out to sea she had sailed. The sun had set; it was growing dark. She was surrounded on all sides by water. The wind had died down. She was becalmed. Her boat rocked gently on the surface of the water next to a buoy. It looked as if she was going to have to tie her sailboat to this floating marker and spend the night out here.

After some time passed she heard the sound of a motor. A spotlight flashed across the water and then a motorboat pulled up beside her. The engine died. A hand reached out of the darkness, grabbing a rope on her sailboat.

A familiar masculine voice exclaimed, "You little idiot! That eggshell you're in isn't made to sail this far into the gulf. Am I going to have to spend the rest of my life rescuing you?"

Her eyes widened. His name was a choked exclamation on her trembling lips. "Grant! What are you doing here? How did you find me?"

"When I got to your houseboat, your neighbor said you'd sailed out of the cove late this afternoon and hadn't gotten back. Here, give me your hand."

He was reaching for her. His strong hand closed over her arm and half lifted her from her little, rocking sailboat onto his big cabin cruiser.